BSJ

The B.S. Johnson Journal

Issue 1, Summer 2014

BSJ: The B.S. Johnson Journal

Editorial

This journal is dedicated to fans, friends, fellow-travellers and finally scholars of the writer B.S. Johnson. If you're reading this, you probably have an idea of who we're talking about. Why else would someone be reading a journal in the internet age?

In *BSJ* we hope to host the best in Johnson-related research alongside original essays, interviews and creative pieces. We feel that - for this issue at least – such hopes have been surpassed. Our featured research papers have been rigorously peer-reviewed by leading Johnson scholars. Fascinating interviews with Zulfikar Ghose and Maureen Duffy provide first-hand accounts of the man they knew so well. The essay section brings fresh takes on Johnson from TV writer extraordinaire David Quantick and Ruth Clemens, a former university student forced into reading *Christie Malry* for her course. Creative pieces from Nick Gadd and Jeremy Page show how Johnson's influence is still inspiring fresh and fertile new writing. We close with a review section in which we review those "writing as though it mattered"; whether that be new Johnson publications, or new writing that Johnson fans might enjoy.

If you wish to contribute something to a future issue of *BSJ: The B.S. Johnson Journal* we would love to hear from you. Send us an email at bsjjournal@gmail.com.

Thank you for reading.

The Editors:

Joseph Darlington

Mark Hooper

Melanie Seddon

Philip Tew

Karen Zouaoui

Contents

B. S. Johnson's *Albert Angelo* as a Postmodern Counterbook

David Leon Higdon

Texas Tech University

In a moment of utter frustration with his teaching job, Albert Angelo
tells Terry, his closest friend, "I was reading this novel recently about a
teacher in the east end who won over kids by love and kindness,
morality and honesty, against tremendous odds—talk about sentiment
and wish-fulfillment!" (*AA,* 130). His following comment immediately
places B. S. Johnson's novel in a new perspective. He continues, "I can
just see my lot coming to me at the end of term with a present—or even
my pen back—addressed *to sir, with their love*" (emphasis added). This
reference, unmistakably specific in nature, establishes *Albert Angelo* as
a counterbook, at term considered below, a parodic reply to E. R.
Braithwaite's hopeful, sentimental, optimistic solution to the problems

in London's schools offered in his quasi-autobiographical *To Sir, With Love.*

In 1941, Jorge Luis Borges, the Argentine author, coined the term *counterbook* in his "Tlön, Uqbar, Orbis Tertius" prophetically anticipating one of the major forms of postmodern fiction: "A book which does not include its opposite, or 'counter-book' is considered incomplete" (*Ficciones,* 29). Earlier in "The Approach to Al-Mu'tasim," he noted "that a present-day book should derive from an ancient one is clearly honorable" (*Ficciones,* 42), and in the much discussed "Pierre Menard, Author of Don Quixote, " the narrator's "general memory of *Don Quixote* . . . is much the same as the imprecise, anterior image of a book not yet written" (*Ficciones,* 51). Some fifty years later, Linda Hutcheon and Fredric Jameson, dissatisfied with the conventional definition of *parody*, took up the inherent challenge in Borges' comments and broadened the concept of the relationship between a text and its counterbook. Hutcheon defined it as "repetition with a critical distance" (*Theory*, xii) and borrowing a term from postmodern architecture, Jameson offered *wrapping* as a term to describe the relationship created when a text such as *To Sir, With Love* is *countered* by *Albert Angelo.* "The kind of parody upon which I wish to focus,"

wrote Hutcheon, "is an integrated structural modeling process of
revising, replaying, inverting, and 'trans-contextualizing' previous
works of art" (*Theory*, 11). Rejecting quotation, intertextuality, and
parody as being inappropriate terms, Jameson proposed that "one text
is simply being wrapped in another . . . The new discourse works hard
to assimilate the 'primary text' . . . into its own substance, transcoding
its elements, foregrounding all the echoes and analogies, sometimes
even borrowing the stylistic features of the illustration in order to forge
the neologisms" (Jameson, 103).

In many ways, *Albert Angelo* is both an aggressive and a
subversive text, because Johnson questions virtually every aspect of *To
Sir, With Love*: its description of school buildings, faculty and
administration, the problems of the protagonist, the handling of tone,
theme, and style, and, especially, its commitment to traditional
concepts of realism. Paradoxically, Johnson offers a realism of
particulars in place of Braithwaite's generalizations. Ultimately, the
conflict between Braithwaite's and Johnson's texts becomes a major
engagement between social realism and postmodernism over what
constitutes an "honest" text. In the early chapters, Braithwaite is quite
particular about details involving buildings and streets, but this

particularity fades as soon as he begins to address people and relationships.

Albert Angelo did not start out as an intertextual reply or even a parody. Indeed, it did not even start out with a character named Albert Angelo, a school setting in London's inner city area, or an exploitation of type and pages. Searching through Johnson's files as he prepared to write *Like a Fiery Elephant*, his biography of Johnson, Jonathan Coe made a most interesting discovery relating to the genesis of the novel. He found a number of pages which were the original introduction Johnson later cancelled, noting that "There was a long section about Graham just here, but I cut it out because Graham bored me . . . I needn't have written it at all. I wasted all that time. And shed no tears because you know little (and will hear no more) of Graham. I assure you he was boring" (quoted in Coe, 445).

Coe does not speculate on what happened to transform this tepid beginning into a rambunctious celebration of the page which would characterize *Albert Angelo*. I speculate the following course. At some point in the early 1960s, Johnson must have read Braithwaite's book and was offended by, even outraged by its old-fashioned form, its easy solutions, and its outdated assumptions about realism, reality, and human psychology. At the same time, though, Johnson probably experienced considerable recognition of kinship. Like Braithwaite, he too had been a supply teacher, he had taught in the inner city schools, he had experienced discipline problems from unruly students, he had been drawn into assessment of the school system, and he was aware of the racial problems. At the same time, he also had a rich stock of incidents and students papers stored away in his memory and his files, but his experiences, however, were virtually opposite to those of Braithwaite's. Between 1960 and 1963, he had lived a "hand-to-mouth" existence (Coe, 92) as a supply teacher, responsible for Maths and Religious Instruction for the Surrey County Council, then the junior school at Baths Pond Road, and finally the Newington Green Junior Modern School. His attitude is partially captured in lines he wrote for a play, *You're Human Like the Rest of Them* (written in October 1964): "Shut up you little bastards, just shut up! / I'm trying to teach you something real, real! Something that I've learnt for myself this time" (quoted in Coe, 177).

Published in 1959, *To Sir, With Love* received an enormous amount of attention, popularity, and endorsement and helped spawn similar books and movies, and the book has gone through at least fifty-one paperback printings in the United States alone. It continues to be considered an *inspirational* and *relevant* book (see *goodreads*). One immediately sees the source of the book's appeal: its problems are simplistically identified; its solutions are spontaneous and easy; and its results are uniformly successful within a very short period of time (actually a compressed nine years, see *RN*, 85). The book hovers ambiguously between autobiography and fiction, combining the two in quite interesting ways and managing to close with a clear-sounding affirmation of human brotherhood while also addressing both educational inadequacies and racism. Its plot is soon told. In 1950-51, Edward Ricardo Braithwaite, a former RAF engineer from British Guiana, takes a job teaching in London's East End. After being demobilized, despite his sterling qualifications, he finds that the color of his skin keeps him from securing appropriate employment in his fields of physics and engineering. Acting on advice from an old man he meets one afternoon in St. James Park, he turns to teaching and quickly secures an appointment teaching fourteen and fifteen year olds at Greenslade School in Stepney. Notice that Braithwaite does not even strive for minimal distancing; he keeps his own name. This raises a considerable number of questions about authenticity, accuracy, and realism. By letting his book be marketed as a *novel*, Braithwaite opened

the door for critics to question the extent to which he exaggerated the

situation; by placing his work firmly within the tradition of

autobiography, Braithwaite attempted to avoid this problem, but, as we

will see, opened more doors for criticism through the tone and

structure he adopted. Several of the early reviews raised issues about

accuracy. E. B., writing in the *New Statesman,* commented that "one is

bound to be embarrassedly uncertain about the degree of

autobiography involved, even to suspect that the author is

compensating for some of the insults and indignities he has endured"

(454). Similar reservations occurred in reviews of the 1964 film of the

book: the protagonist, one reviewer notes, "is heroic yet human at the

same time," but said the movie "comes off as a cozy, good-humoured

and unbelievable little tale . . . implying but never-stating that it is nice

for the races to live congenially together" (Crowther, 24).

Braithwaite's school may be lightly fictionalized; its location is

not. Greenslade in the Stepney/Limehouse/Shadwell area, the East End

Cockney area of London, still showed extensive damage from wartime

bombing as late as 1964. The school "overlooked the gutted remains of

a bomb-wrecked church, squatting among a mixture of gravestones and rubble" (*TS*, 17) and rises "out of a courtyard, a solid, unpretentious, rather dirty structure, no taller than its neighbors" (*TS*, 18). Its headmaster emphasizes to Braithwaite that many of the difficulties within the school are endemic, because "[t]he children in this area have always been poorly fed, clothed and housed. By the very nature of their environment they are subject to many pressures and tensions which tend to inhibit their spiritual, moral and physical growth" (*TS*, 29). Problems are indeed rife within this unpromising building. The students' clothing, like themselves, is dirty; there is little in the way of discipline or hygiene; few students seem to care about learning anything the school offers; the students are shockingly vulgar, coarse, violent, and hostile to their teachers. Some of the teachers are equally hostile to the students, or, perhaps worse, utterly indifferent. Mixed nationalities and mixed races exacerbate the tensions, and the sullen energies of this new generation find outlets only in the noonday dancing sessions. Snatched cigarettes in the toilets, none too innocent petting in the halls, and "teacher-baiting" are the daily challenges to civilized discipline. The students would not agree with Prime Minister Harold Macmillan's remark that "most of our people have never had it so good" (Britons).

Braithwaite's book told its English speaking audience what it wanted to hear: namely, that a caring, dedicated, firm teacher could transform undisciplined juvenile delinquents into responsive students and promising citizens. Their Dionysian energies and excesses could be channeled in socially useful ways and molded into acceptable forms, and the solutions lay in individuals, not in expensive new programs. The reviews, while not glossing over problems with the book, were enthusiastic on both sides of the Atlantic, almost breathing a sigh of relief that solutions for the "school crisis" were at hand. The London *Times Literary Supplement* called the book "apposite at the moment with its intelligent descriptions of race discrimination" (*Times*, 194). In *The New Yorker*. John McCanten was more colloquial, praising "the combination of firmness and flexible good sense by which he managed to tame the embryo Teddy boys and precocious slatterns who made up his class . . . An engaging and most instructive memoir" (McCarten 120). Typical of many reviewers, Judith Crist found the book to be "a heartwarming and inspiring contrast to the gangbuster and sensational type of writing we have recently had about America's educational problems . . . his narrative shines with simplicity and frankness and, understandably, with occasional flashes of self-righteousness" (Crist,

8). Over all, most reviewers found Braithwaite's book "a moving and genuinely inspirational account," and "a tender, warm, hopeful autobiographical fragment that demonstrates the need for the young to be treated with mature interest and made to measure up to objective standards" (Byam, 754). *Time* praised Braithwaite's victory over his "hard and gutterwise" students through his realization that "the quality of the teacher is far more important than the strictness, or permissiveness of the school" ("Slum School").

Braithwaite (the character) is a romantic idealist who has imbibed the dream of British democracy and tolerance from a distance and from books. As he rides the bus along Commercial Road for the first time, he thinks: "I had entertained some naively romantic ideas about London's East End, with its cosmopolitan population and fascinating history. I had read references to it in both classical and contemporary writings and was eager to know the London of Chaucer and Erasmus and the Sorores Minores. I had dreamed of walking along the cobbled Street of the Cable Makers ... I had dreamed" (*TS,* 9), but as with myriad other dreamers, reality brings him up short: "There was nothing romantic about the noisy littered street bordered by an untidy irregular picket fence of slipshod shopfronts and gaping bomb sites ...

The few remaining buildings, raped and outraged, were still partly

occupied, the missing glass panes replaced by clapboard, or bright

colored squares of tinplate . . . There was rubble everywhere, and dirt

and flies. And there were smells" (*TS*, 9). The school brings the same

shocking contrast. "My vision of teaching in a school was one of

straight rows of desks, and neat, well-mannered, obedient children.

The room I had just left seemed like a menagerie" (*TS*, 14). Daily his

students test his mettle, first with the silent treatment, then with the

noisy treatment, and finally with the "bawdy" treatment. His initial

"effervescence of spirit" (*TS*, 32) is assaulted on every side by the size of

his class (forty-six students), and their vulgar unresponsiveness and

"very sullenness . . . assumed in and out of school like a kind of armor; a

gesture against authority; a symbol of toughness as thin and synthetic

as the cheap films [probably the adaptation of Evan Hunter's *The*

Blackboard Jungle] from which it was copied" (*TS*, 51) bring him to the

brink of defeat. His solution—one many adults of the day

enthusiastically endorsed—"tough love." He announces new and non-

negotiable guidelines, while appealing to the students' sense of their

nearing futures as wage-earning individuals: "My business here is to

teach you, and I shall do my best to make my teaching as interesting as possible. . . . Most of you will be leaving school within six months or so;

that means that in a short while you will be embarked on the very adult

business of earning a living. Bearing that in mind, I have decided that

from now on you will be treated not as children, but as young men and

women, by me and by each other. When we move out of the state of

childhood certain higher standards of conduct are expected of us . . ."

(*TS*, 72-73). These guidelines have an almost immediate effect on the

students' forms of address, deportment, hygiene, and scholastic

attitude. The students continue to test him, but his victories come with

almost unearned ease. An anonymous contemporary Head of Science

in a London school generally commented that "the minute you look

upon your pupils as difficult you start thinking of them as unteachable .

. . To be involved in the classroom is to understand that our pupils are

teachable and highly intelligent. At the moment, however, there is *no*

belief in the ability of our pupils at all" (quoted in Grace, 179). After

showing his interest and trust by taking his students on a visit to the

Victoria and Albert Museum, he finds a vase of flowers on his desk.

Braithwaite moves steadily and progressively once he has announced

the principles of the new regime. Initially, he and the students spar

tentatively over power and dominance, but after his moment of decision, "I had an idea" (*TS*, 72), and his defeat of Denham in the boxing ring during a physical exercise session; no disciplinary problems disrupt his classroom. The visit to the museum is followed shortly by field trips to Sadler Wells, the Old Vic, and Wembley Stadium as part of his primary agenda of teaching his students basic humanity rather than specific subjects. His first major victory comes when two of his students report to the entire school on their work. Moira Joseph reports that the lessons have "had a particular bias toward the brotherhood of mankind" (*TS*, 138), and Fernman, the class clown in some ways, uses the school skeleton to amuse and to show that "basically all people were the same; the trimmings might be different but the foundations were all laid out according to the same blueprint" (*TS*, 139).

The generalities of this lesson, however, are difficult for his students to translate into particulars. When Larry Seales' mother dies, the students tell their teacher they cannot attend the funeral because the household is racially mixed. When Moira Jackson tells Braithwaite, "'It's what people would say if they saw us going to a colored person's home'" (*TS*, 169), Braithwaite feels defeated one more time by the unvoiced but constantly present racial prejudices of the area and the culture. When he arrives at the funeral and finds all his class in

attendance, though, he is reduced to tears. *To Sir, With Love* plays the

rhythm of the advances in the classroom against the setbacks outside

the school to validate Braithwaite's vision and approach. We only find

out much later that the lessons did not stick with all his students.

Braithwaite tells his readers in *Reluctant Neighbors* (1972) that one of

his first students, a "well-developed blonde with the large green eyes

whom the others nicknamed Droopy" (*RN*, 92), saw him on the street

one day and crossed over to avoid having to speak with him.

Episodic developments of his experiences at Greenslade

become flaws which demonstrate exactly what qualities on

Braithwaite's pages would drive B. S. Johnson to attack *To Sir, With*

Love. Braithwaite goes from victory to victory within the classroom;

serious threats always come from without and almost never endanger

the classroom itself—Patrick Fernman's arrest, Mrs. Dare's "dating," the

racist waiter at Poisson d'Or, and the death of Larry Seales' mother.

When there is trouble in his classroom, Braithwaite intervenes and

deftly solves the problem, as when he handles the Buckley bullying

incident in Bell's physical education class. A certain smugness creeps

into the comments, as when Braithwaite remembers the conditions of the area where he taught. "I found myself thinking of the old days when elderly people in the East End of London reached forward to shake hands with me, just for the luck which they believed would result" (*PS,* 145). He feels he has become an icon to the people of Stepney. At least four features of *To Sir, With Love* cited earlier probably antagonised Johnson because they so violated what he wished to practice in writing fiction: its self-congratulatory tone, its smug assumptions about teenagers, its "outdated" ideological realism, and its distance from the world of books.

To B. S. Johnson, Braithwaite's decision to record what had happened exactly as it had happened was an abnegation of the demands of art. Whether as comic aside or bold statement, Johnson and Albert Angelo believe art's primary task is to shape, to form, even to subjugate life and facts into a pattern. Urinating in Grace's Alley, for instance, Albert "[n]ever content to leave well alone, . . . unzipped his fly and attempted to impose the pattern of art on nature" (*AA,* 125), and in key passages first Albert and then Johnson stress the absolute necessity of squeezing meaning and form out of life. In keeping with his interest in architectural form and design, Albert thinks that "there was this tremendous need for man to impose a pattern on life . . . Inanimate life is always moving towards disintegration, towards chaos, and man is

moving in the opposite direction, towards the imposition of order" (*AA*,

133); and Johnson, agreeing for once with his character, notes that

"faced with the enormous detail, vitality, size, of this complexity, of life,

there is a great temptation for a writer to impose his own pattern, an

arbitrary pattern which must falsify, cannot do anything other than

falsify" (*AA*, 170). Johnson even has a blind man trump Braithwaite's

racial theme by having him tell Albert, "you've got to be black today:

you're better thought of" (*AA*, 124). Thus the smugness of tone, the

uninterrupted chain of accomplishments, the "flatearther" style, and the

unstructured episodes featured prominently in *To Sir, with Love* are the

very qualities which so provoked Johnson into entering into a debate,

an argument, a refutation about what was "real" and "not real" in

London's inner city, the psychology of school children, and the fast

changing milieu of the 1950s and 1960s. As Johnson comments in the

"Introduction" to *Aren't You Rather Young to Be Writing Your Memoirs?*,

"Life does not tell stories. Life is chaotic, fluid, random; it leaves

myriads of ends untied, untidily. Writers can extract a story from life

only by strict, close selection, and this must mean falsification" (*AY*, 14).

But is *To Sir, With Love* a truthful book? Would its

methodology actually work in the hands of other teachers at other

schools? Does it record an overly optimistic victory of a particular

ideology over actualities? B. S. Johnson certainly felt that the book,

however well intended, however well planned, simply romanticized the

situation and probably contributed more to increasing problems than

to finding solutions. He does not foreground and publicly exploit the

key intertextual connection but rather places it late in his novel and

offers it in such a way that his reader should experience an epiphany, a

moment of recognition which not only sheds new light on what has

gone before but emphatically on what comes after. The reference

suddenly traps the reading within a framework of unexpected meaning.

Braithwaite and Johnson stand on opposite sides of a divide,

separated by culture, nationality, race, attitudes towards their students,

assumptions about what can be accomplished in the classroom and

then recaptured by art clash repeatedly. Johnson stands significantly

apart because of a philosophical and aesthetic divide. The divide

between movements, styles, and ages is seldom as pronounced in

literature as it is for some other disciplines; however, critics discern a

sharp line through British fiction of the late 1950s and early 1960s. On the one side stand the accomplishments of engaged social realism, the

novels of George Orwell, Alan Sillitoe, Kingsley Amis, John Braine, John

Wain, and others, not to mention many of the earlier novels of L. P.

Hartley, Graham Greene, Evelyn Waugh, and Aldous Huxley, who in

work after work from the early 1920s extending into the 1960s

identified the problems affecting the individual, the society, the

government, and the culture of Great Britain, and who suggested

numerous solutions for reshaping government, for reaffirming the

spiritual dimension of being, and for challenging youthful rebellion. A

new fictional world was coming into being after World War II, and

novelists wanted to have a clear say in what this world should be.

In the early 1960s, social realism began to be displaced by

postmodernism, as is clearly evident in the style, form, and intention of

three works: Anthony Burgess's *A Clockwork Orange* (1962), John

Fowles's *The Collector* (1963), and Johnson's *Albert Angelo* (1964).

Superficially, these novels may appear to belong to the social realism

movement. Burgess explored adolescent violence and the price of

disciplining thuggish youth in order to make an ordered society

possible. His Alex resembles Sillitoe's Arthur Seaton, though his

antisocial behavior goes far beyond Arthur's drunkenness, fights, sexual exploits, and car-tipping. Fowles's Frederick Clegg belongs to the long

tradition of the psychopath, questioning whether genes or environment

have turned a butterfly collector into a sadistic modern Bluebeard, and

Johnson's Albert, a bungling, incompetent substitute teacher is akin to

Amis's Jim Dixon and Wain's Charles Lumley. No reader, however,

would mistake these three works for socially conscious, socially

committed works. By foregrounding language play and its strikingly

symmetrical sonata structure, *A Clockwork Orange* announces its

primary concern with the shapes, sounds, puns, and multiple meanings

of its medium. By focusing on the polytonal intermeshing of narrative

voices and making the victim's musings philosophical, Fowles

generalizes his work into an existential fable. By running roughshod

over every aspect of earlier literary decorum, leaving holes in pages,

and framing the entire novel with a long epigraph from Samuel

Beckett's *The Unnamable*, Johnson aligns himself with such earlier

works as Laurence Sterne's *Tristram Shandy*, skipping over all the

social and novelistic conventions of his contemporaries and the

Victorians.

  The satire and parody of schools in the novels of Charles

Dickens, Charlotte Brontë, and William Makepeace Thackeray in the

1840s indirectly prepared the way for the contrast between the works of Braithwaite and Johnson, and the divide in literary movements keenly sharpened this contrast. Johnson's parody is a forthright, bold challenge to Braithwaite's *To Sir, With Love* on its many grounded aspects—geography, description, clothing styles, teenage toughness, East End culture, even subplot. *Albert Angelo* is far more aggressively accurate geographically, topographically, sociologically, and linguistically. Percy Circus, where Albert Angelo lives, is detailed quite specifically, still as accurate in 1991 when I explored the area as it was for Johnson in 1964. One could still walk from Percy Circus to King's Cross Station exactly following Albert Angelo's steps because numerous businesses named in 1964 were still there in the 1990s, though Number 29 Percy Circus, the site of Albert's flat, had long been a vacant lot, a necessary absence into which Johnson could pour his fictive character. Twenty-nine is Albert's "favourite number" [*AA*, 132], the number he punches on the jukebox, the age he is approaching, and possibly the number defining his generation's manta of "trust no one over thirty," because he once refers to "an old woman of about thirty" [*AA*, 37].

When Albert's students speak, they little resemble Braithwaite's students sliding into the idiomatic "bleedin'." About the most extreme we see in Braithwaite's pages is Pamela Dare commenting "'Daft, that's what you are, the lot of youse, daft, stupid, soft!'" (*TS*, 108); elsewhere, their language is described merely as "expressed without rigid observation for the rules of syntax" (*TS*, 112). When Albert's students talk, their utterances are recorded very accurately, even shockingly so: "'Ere, sir, d'you know some boy, 'e said there was a pole frough the norf and souf poles!'" (*AA*, 44), or "Albie'll 'ave t' go if 'e's goin' t' be like this all the time, e'll 'ave t' go?'" (*AA*, 69), and the reader is actually allowed to see their written exercises. Johnson drives home the lack of even the most basic skills: "The weding of our beloved Mr Alburt he was going to get marred to miss Croswait on the night befor he got parerlatick drunk to buck up inogth corag to say Yes. On the day they got marred he was sick twic" (*AA*, 122), and "he gives us good lessons sometimes I feel like swearing at him . . . There's on thing wrong with him he needs a haricut. And one thing more he rekcons his self to much he gose round the class punching us for nothing and on Friday night I am going to break his Stick" (*AA*, 163). Moreover, his students are much more destructive and malicious. They "befoul" his valuable edition of Paul Frankl's *The Gothic: Literary Sources and Interpretations through Eight Centuries*, which he reads in class to forget his students, steal his personal pen, dump used condoms in his wastebasket, and discolor the sample of gneiss he lets them hold (a chunk of Irish gneiss which has intense connections to his broken love affair). In turn, Albert raps out corporal punishment (which is forbidden), lectures them on the possible non-existence of God (which is legally forbidden), bores them with geology lessons, and finally detaches himself as far as possible from his classroom. The students, after all, have already scored one goal: they have driven his predecessor to suicide and tell Albert "We're going to have a meeting tonight to decide about you" (*AA*, 128). As Albert tells his friend Terry, "It's like I'm working at the frontiers of civilisation all the time" (*AA*, 132).

Braithwaite and Johnson present their protagonists in three contexts: the classroom, the teacher's lounge, and the private world, the latter two intended to contrast with the former. The teacher's lounge scenes enable the authors to play views on education and on students off against one another; the private world enables them to show their protagonists in relationships with friends and girlfriends. Braithwaite finds himself surrounded with a humanitarian principal and teachers keenly interested in the well-being of their students, but they have been worn down with the effort of teaching difficult students. The teacher's lounge in *To Sir, with Love* is more a refuge for coffee, tea, and snacks than for debate over educational policy. Mostly, the teachers advise Braithwaite not to be too hard on the students because "they mean no harm, really; they're not bad when you get to know them" (*TS*, 61). While Braithwaite considers his agenda in private, talking it over only with his "foster" Mom and Dad, Albert simply flails about in isolation. Albert, though, is seen against the backdrop of three schools, teaching students of different ages. He begins at St. Sepulchre's for a few days, teaching nine and ten year olds, several of whom speak little or no English. At this stage, he enjoys teaching; indeed as he walks to school, he thinks: "You look forward to teaching. You think of it as a very great privilege, to be allowed to work amongst children. Very worthwhile, very satisfying" (*AA*, 41). He is almost immediately transferred to Wormwood Street Junior Boys' School in the shadows of Liverpool Street Station, where the "modern method" is in effect. Two days later he is at Crane Grove Secondary School, with forty-six fourteen year olds, perhaps the most challenging of adolescent ages, and the problems which peel away his idealism layer by layer, leaving him only distrust and fear of his students.

Both Braithwaite and Albert are displaced persons, alienated from their chosen disciplines. Braithwaite is centered, confident, and fully grounded in himself, whether in his classroom or in his courtship of Gillian Blanchard who ultimately disappears into silence. In the spirit of parody, Albert is utterly neurotic. Four and a half years earlier Jenny, Albert's love, "betrayed" Albert for a physically crippled man rather than stay in a relationship with the emotionally crippled Albert. Albert truly deserves the label *born loser*. A twenty-eight year old man with college training in architecture, his own flat, and an income creates certain horizons of expectation in the 1960s—a satisfying job, a fairly confident sense of self, an active dating and sex life, plans for the future. Albert has none of these, even though, in many ways, he is a true man of the 1960s with his long blond hair (as frequently remarked in students' weekly reviews), his suede shoes, his sloppy shirt and pants; however, Albert has been psychologically wounded and cannot bring himself to stop twisting the knife in the wound. His disillusionment turns him misogynistic: "Snares, delusions, frauds, women" (*AA*, 110); virtually impotent: "Because Jenny was so good, so what I wanted, anyway, that I can't bring myself to, for money, nor can I love anyone else" (*AA*, 113); and cynical to the point that one character tells him, "You're just using her as an excuse. You could forget these things easily enough if you didn't bloody think so much about them" (*AA*, 145). He has abandoned architecture, a subject that yet holds him closely, so that he can punish himself by being a part-time substitute teacher, a punishment that he feels will eventually make him once again worthy of Jenny. He even frames his pain with grandiose allusions to Shakespeare's Hamlet and Milton's Satan.

His classroom battle culminates not in a heartfelt offered gift, but in a death and a total victory for the students, the very opposite of Braithwaite's victory. In the novel's "Coda," five of Albert's students, who call themselves The Corps, encounter Albert as he walks along Colebrooke Row, near the Angel Pub and Vincent Terrace, on his way back to Percy Circus. They toss him into the canal over which Colebrooke Row crosses and watch him drown. The novel then closes with a parody of Braithwaite's humanitarian victory, the funeral with all his students in attendance, as an affirmation of their friendship with Seales and in sympathy for his mother. *Albert Angelo* ends with a very different and "shocking display of funeralization" (*AA*, 180), but the corpse is not Albert's; rather it is a friend's mother who has "pastaway" (*AA*, 180). The girl, in whose inarticulate and illiterate voice the final paragraph is written, concludes: "A funeral is rather a nastey thing it always makes me come out in goospimples and all cold when i herd my big sisters friends mama pastaway . . . Just plan stupid two spend and wast all that money on a thing like that it was Just a gerate wast of time and all that work fore relley nothing Just a shocking display of funeralization on behalf of the furm that was calld in" (*AA*, 180).

Much more separates the two books than a dialogic debate over whether or not inner city fourteen year olds can be educated and civilized by tough love and treating them as young adults. Braithwaite maintains they can; Johnson offers a blunt, violent rejoinder. Despite their shared interests in realistically portraying the students, their environment, their speech patterns, and their futures, no one could mistake the two works as belonging to the same period or style. *To Sir With Love* follows decorum strictly and emerges as a work uniform in every respect. Transparent style, consistent perspective, uniform focalization, and insistent foregrounding of social problems mark Braithwaite's book as an old-fashioned, socially purposed, didactic novel. With Johnson's novel, we are in the fictional equivalent of the miniskirt, the Carnaby Street tie, rock 'n roll, long hair for males—in other words, fully in an early postmodern insouciant reply. Johnson is not content to simply mount an argument against Braithwaite's arguments; he assaults the very assumptions which underpin each and every one of its twenty-two chapters. Because Johnson assigns Braithwaite to the category "literary flatearthers," the two works part company at the level of the page. *Albert Angelo* rebels against the traditional page by offering several newly invented punctuation marks (to distinguish speech from thought, for example), breaking its pages into columns of public and private action, spacing words oddly, and finally culminating its romp with holes in pages 149-52, a device which caused Australian censors to confiscate the novel, feeling that something "obscene" had been razored out by the importer who planned to paste it back in once the book cleared customs (*AY*, 31). The device lets Johnson mislead his readers (not for the first time) by juxtaposing the threats against Albert's life with a violent stabbing death partially glimpsed through the holes. A reader turns the pages expecting every moment to have his assumptions about Albert's murder confirmed, only to discover that he/she has read about Christopher Marlowe's murder. And, if one looks backwards through the holes, one sees only blank space, the blankness of the nil.

Braithwaite would have regarded all such devices as distractions

endangering the social purpose of the book. Johnson more

emphatically stresses the fictionality and detailed realism of his novel

and the presence of the author, primarily through the selection of the

Samuel Beckett epigraph, the table of contents made up of conceptual

terms, the quotations of bizarrely unrelated documents, such as the

business card picked up from the sidewalk or the eighteenth-century

anatomy text unexpectedly cited at one point, and a polemical

disclaimer which forces one into a dialogue over the artist as teacher

versus the artist as architect, the engagement of the social activist

versus the self-reflexiveness of the postmodern writer.

Johnson's novel concedes that Braithwaite advances a pictorial,

documentary realism in describing the general setting, the physical

condition of the buildings, and, especially, the physical objects, though

he objects to the generalization of these. Whereas Braithwaite simply

opens a drawer, Albert not only opens a drawer, but takes a quick

census of its contents—as any experienced teacher would do: "Under

the register and the dinner book is a litter of school-children's

valuables: marbles, sweets, plastic whistles, a spring balance, razorblades, three thimbles, handkerchiefs, keys, chewed rubbers, brushes, pens, pencils, useless plastic parts, ballpen refills, cereal manufacturers' lures, a Durex packet, and a long blunt sheathknife" (*AA,* 32). Where Braithwaite, watching students listen to Chopin's *Fantasie Impromptu* and part of Vivaldi's *Concerto in C for two trumpets,* notices the students "were listening, actively, attentively listening to those records, with the same raptness they had shown in the jiving" (*TS,* 52), Albert witnesses a true moment of epiphany in one student: "when we got to the phrase 'Da mi basia' repeated several times with increasing passion, this little Greek Cypriot girl suddenly sat up, said 'Oh!' and smiled all over her face... so at least I pleased one of them that day, though god knows if she understood any of the rest" (*AA,* 131). Braithwaite's decorous notice of a fellow teacher's "prominent breasts clamor[ing] for attention" (*TS,* 19) becomes a running joke in *Albert Angelo* as "the monumental mammaries" and "lovely big tits" (*AA,* 105) of Miss Crosswaithe, whose name obviously echoes Braithwaite's. Johnson eschews the generalities Braithwaite offers his reader. Braithwaite's prose is a realism of surfaces and general comments only, because his observations have no psychological realism or depth, except when they are concerned with the protagonist himself, and have only an ideological commitment to Victorian style realism.

Paradoxically, the theoretical comments of both Albert and Johnson

show that Johnson approached realism through an almost photographic

style, detailing and patterning where Braithwaite patterned and then

generalised.

A fifth objection could have been added to Johnson's earlier

objections had he read Braithwaite's final book, *Reluctant Neighbors*,

which rehearses Braithwaite's life from the 1940s until the 1970s and

tells how each of his books came to be written. *Reluctant Neighbors*

seethes with racial anger and in many ways is the most interesting of

Braithwaite's works. The "reluctant neighbors" are Braithwaite and a

stockbroker who happen to be sitting next to one another on the train

one morning as it carries them into the heart of Manhattan.

Conversation, somewhat unwillingly, ensues. Because the conversation

sparks flashbacks to the actual incidents in his life, Braithwaite recalls

just how he wrote *To Sir, with Love* and claims this authenticates the

documentary reality of his work. He reveals that he kept a "laboriously

compiled record of nine years of teaching . . . The records stared me in

the face, mocking me. I had written about my pupils, arguing with

myself that I was observing them, looking squarely at them, learning from them" (*RN*, 85). He was rereading and talking about these notebooks when his "Mom" suggested, indeed insisted, that he turn them into a book of some kind. Her simple question, "Why don't you put it all together into a book?" (*RN*, 88) was all the motivation he needed. Soon he had bought typing paper, rented a typewriter, and set up a card table under the apple tree in their back yard. He "took the notebooks and beginning from page one of book number one, typed what I had written down. All of it" (*RN*, 89). Soon the pages mounted up; he had them bound and took the title from the inscription his students had written on gift paper. As is evident, though, he admits he collapsed nine years of experience and records into one school year, and undoubtedly omitted and combined.

Braithwaite's arranged copying of real events and real people utilizing such compression would have struck Johnson as "false art," if indeed art at all. In his introduction to *Aren't You Rather Young to be Writing Your Memoirs?* Johnson denounced such writing, suggesting that it was as ancient and outdated and invalid as the Ptolemaic system. He argued that simply repeating the modes and methods of earlier art, especially in a period when motion pictures had antiquated many things novels still attempted to do, was an act of narrative cowardice.

Ironically, the same point was being argued by Alain Robbe-Grillet in the work regarded as the theoretical backbone of the *noveau roman* school, where he rejected "several obsolete notions" such as character, story, and realism, arguing that each generation must "reinvent" the novel (*Nouveau*, 25). In the introduction to *Aren't You Rather Young to be Writing Your Memoirs?*, Johnson recalled that "I really discovered what I should be doing with *Albert Angelo* . . . where I broke through the English disease of the objective correlative to speak truth directly if solipsistically in the novel form, and heard my own small voice" (*AY*, 22). He prided himself on being able to play with the page and approach reality from oblique angles rather than head-on as had Braithwaite. He rejected the mirror theory of realism which had dominated so much nineteenth century and social realist writing. Johnson treated Braithwaite's work as a book which invites another book in reply, and he frees this book from the imprisonment of *To Sir, With Love* in the form of *Albert Angelo*, thus fulfilling Jorge Luis Borges' comment of 1941 that "A book which does not include its opposite, or 'counter-book' is considered incomplete" (Borges, 29). As Johnson wrote in *Travelling People*, "I should be determined not to lead my reader into believing that he was doing anything but reading a novel, having noted with abhorrence the shabby chicanery practiced on their readers by many novelists, particularly of the popular class" (*TP*, 21), all of this in service of his credo that life is chaotic; art is form. It was on these several grounds that Johnson decided to confront Braithwaite's work. He simply believed that its claims to reality were falsified and sentimentalized—it seems difficult to disagree—and that its claims should be impugned by turning its positive images into negative images.

Whereas *To Sir, With Love* studiously, almost monkishly, avoids extratextual references, *Albert Angel* is a very bookish novel which not only limns its pages with references but which fully exploits these references for the good of the book. The references have quite different purposes in their authority and source—whether, that is, they originate with the protagonist, another character, or the author. Albert, for example, appropriates images and lines from Shakespeare, Milton, Shelley, and others, which ultimately emphasize his egotism, his sense of defeat, and his role-playing. The results are quite often hilarious as when he cites *Hamlet*'s Bernardo's "For this relief much thanks, much thanks!" (*AA*, 102), to express his simultaneous gratitude for a completely satisfying ejaculation and recognition that the new day is a school holiday. Within moments, though, he alludes to Satan in *Paradise Lost* as he thinks about his lost Jenny: "even though it's four and a half years since, now, four and a half long years of my selfmade hell, though, what the hell is hell, it's another of those meaningless words like sin or evil or god. Nor am I out of it" (*AA*, 102). He returns several times to Hamlet's "recchy kisses" (*AA*, 145, 149) and Milton again when he asserts that he cannot explain the ways of women to man (*AA*, 144). Where Albert uses only references and allusions, Johnson turns them into intertexts, especially through the Beckett epigraph, the Petronius reference (*AA*, 138), the citation of Terence (*AA*, 169), and, of course, the Braithwaite quotation.

Immediately following the sudden and unexpected "almighty aposiopesis" (*AA*, 167), a voice intermediary between Albert and Johnson, cries out, "Im trying to say something not tell a story telling stories is telling lies and I want to tell the truth about me about my experience about my truth about my truth to reality about sitting here writing looking out across Claremont Square trying to say something about the writing and nothing being an answer to the loneliness to the lack of loving" (*AA*, 167-68). We can clearly see that Braithwaite is an early version of the formerly idealistic Albert Angelo, and, in addition, that Albert is a version of a version of Johnson himself.

These passages clarify not only the relationship between Albert and Johnson, but also Johnson's perceptions of the ties in the series of the teachers. They stand as repetitions of a type separated by the educational, social, racial, and political lens of the authors. Braithwaite launched the same quasi-autobiographical, melodramatic statement which Evan Hunter used in *Blackboard Jungle*, and for better or worse, helped focus the dialogue on both sides of the Atlantic about educational programs and standards for the next decade and beyond. Johnson's contribution to the dialogue not only is his trenchant parody but also his merging the dialogue back into the realm of fiction. He will have none of the artifices of realism found in Braithwaite's compression of nine calendar years into one school year, because his own particularised, detailed realism demonstrates what Braithwaite must have left out.

Johnson boldly plays on this ambiguity when, in the "almighty aposiopesis" (*AA*, 167), he renounces the realities of his pages: "fuck all this lying look what im really trying to write about is writing not all this stuff about architecture trying to say something about writing about my writing im my hero though what a useless appellation my first

character then im trying to say something about me through him" (*AA,*

167). Albert looks out over Percy Circus, the fictional narrator over

Claremont Square, and Johnson himself over Marchmount Square.

Johnson gives us a postmodern image of receding but connected males.

Just as Percy Circus fades into Claremont Square and then into

Marchmount Square, Albert fades into the implied author and then into

Johnson himself. Quickly, we see a Shakespearean play within a play

within a play device develop before us in which the highly fictionalized

world of Albert Angelo becomes into the "lived" world of the "author"

and emphatically disappears into the actual world of B. S. Johnson

himself. The "author" tells his reader that the novel contains several

agendas, giving the novel almost a reflexive ending in which alternate

interpretations are posed. The first aim is didactic: "the novel must be

a vehicle for conveying truth, and to this end every device and

technique of the printer's art should be at the command of the writer"

(*AA,* 175). Second stands "social comment on teaching, to draw

attention, too, to improve: but with less hope, for if the government

wanted better education it could be provided easily enough" (*AA,* 176);

and finally, "Oh, and there were some pretty parallels to be drawn between build-on-the-skew, tatty, half-complete comically-called Percy

Circus, and Albert, and London, and England, and the human condition"

(*AA,* 176), hinting at numerous textual layers of allegory. Braithwaite

accepted the didactic role, but only the didactic role and saw his

primary task as advancing a pedagogical method and educating the

English world about the strong current of racism surging beneath its

noble abstractions. David Lodge's *Spectator* review concluded that "the

fact that Mr. Johnson can tease us with such provocative questions

about the relation of art to reality is an indication and of his talent and

of his promise" (Lodge, 117). In terms of the popularity and impact of

To Sir, With Love and its motion picture adaptation, Braithwaite may

have won a victory with the public on both sides of the Atlantic;

however, *Albert Angelo,* aligning itself with the images of *Blackboard*

Jungle, restored the dialogue over the conditions of schools to the

darkness, violence, and failures of the classroom.

Ironically, late 1964 saw the publication of another school

novel which seemed largely to expand and validate Johnson's take on

postmodern realism and which also took even more Johnsonian

liberties with the page. Bel Kaufman's *Up the Down Stair Case* offers the

reader "a composite of all the schools in which [she] had taught" (*UDSC,*

xv) which "juxtaposed . . . chaos, confusion, cries for help, bureaucratic

gobbledygook and one teacher's attempt to make a difference in the life

of one youngster" (*UDSC,* xii). Kaufman's book stands just a bit later

than the dialogue between Braithwaite and Johnson, intersecting with

their works. As fully aware of the school problems being discussed in

newspapers, magazines, and reports in the 1950s and early 1960s, she

took as her target a "school system... strangulated by its own red tape ...

mired in rigidity and befogged by empty rhetoric" (*UDSC,* xxiv). More

than numerous other authors, Kaufman lets her students and their

parents speak in their own voices, and where Braithwaite would chide

her lack of social vision, Johnson would praise the postmodern

bricolage constantly evident on her pages as she gathers memos,

student papers and comments, official reports, and drawings.

Kaufman's book is an eccentric compilation, ambiguously poised

between social realism and postmodernism. Johnson's *Albert Angelo*

stands emphatically as one of the most successful of the counterbook

phenomenon which characterizes postmodernism's restatement of a

previous text but in a much different key, rhythm, and style.

Endnote

[1] The abbreviations for the novels discussed in the essay are: for E. R. Braithwaite, *RN* (*Reluctant Neighbors*), *TS* (*To Sir, with Love*); for B. S. Johnson, *AA* (*Albert Angelo*), *AY* (*Aren't You Rather Young to be Writing Your Memoirs?*), and *TP* (*Travelling People*); for Bel Kaufman, *UDSC* (*Up the Down Staircase*).

Works Cited

B., E. "Review: *To Sir, with Love.*" *New Statesman* 57 (28 March 1959): 454.

Braithwaite, E. R. *Reluctant Neighbors.* New York: McGraw-Hill, 1972.

---. *To Sir, with Love.* New York: Jove Books, 1977.

"Britons 'have never had it so good'."
(http://news.bbc.co.uk/onthisday/hi/dates/stories/July20/newsed-37280000.3728225.stm).

Byam, M. S. "Review: *To Sir, with Love.*" *Library Journal* 85 (15 February 1960): 754.

Coe, Jonathan. *Like a Fiery Elephant.* New York: Continuum, 2005.

Crist, Judith. "Review: *To Sir, with Love.*" *New York Herald Tribune Book Review*, 28 February 1960, 8.

Crowther, Bosley. "Defense: Knowledge is Power." *Time* 70 (18

November 1957), 21-24.

Goodreads: *To Sir, with Love*

(http://www.goodreads.com/book/show/895163.html.)

Grace, Gerald. *Teachers, Ideology and Control: A Study in Urban
Education*. London: Routledge & Kegan Paul, 1978.

Hunter, Evan. *The Blackboard Jungle*. Cambridge, MA: Robert Bentley,
1954.

Johnson, B. S. *Albert Angelo*. New York: New Directions, 1987.

---. *Aren't You Rather Young to Be Writing Your Memoirs?* London:
Hutchinson, 1973.

---. *Travelling People*. London: Constable, 1963.

Kaufman, Bel. *Up the Down Stair Case*. New York: Harper Perennial,
1991.

Lodge, David. "Tilting the Camera: Review of *Albert Angelo*." *Spectator*
24 July 1964.

McCarten, John. "Cinema: Not to the Tune of a Hickory Stick." *New
Yorker* 31 (26 March 1955): 120.

McCourt, Frank. *Teacher Man*. New York: Scribner, 2005.

"Review: *To Sir, with Love*." *Times Literary Supplement*, 3 April 1959,
194.

Robbe-Grillet, Alain. *For a New Novel*. Trans. Richard Howard. New

York: Grove Press, 1965.

"Slum School." *Time*, 11 July 1959, 66.

A Foucauldian Analysis of Disciplinary Power, Disease and

Bodily Decay in *House Mother Normal*

Kate Connolly

University of Glasgow

In *Discipline and Punish*, Michel Foucault argues that systems of control

and punishment commonly used in prisons are to be found in

institutions everywhere, for example, in offices, factories, schools and

hospitals. These institutions share the same basic structures and use

rigid timetables to control both the space occupied by individuals

within them and the use of their time, hour by hour.

> Gradually, an administrative and political space was
> articulated upon a therapeutic space; it tended to individualise
> bodies, diseases, symptoms, lives and deaths; it constituted a
> real table of juxtaposed and carefully distinct singularities. Out
> of discipline, a medically useful space was born (Foucault,
> *Discipline and Punish*, 144).

As Foucault asserts in *Discipline and Punish*, the carceral system extends everywhere in society, creating obedient subjects, "subjected and practised bodies, 'docile' bodies" (138). For Foucault, this applied to both the physical reality of an institution such as a hospital and to the specific discourses that proliferate around the workings of the institution, such as the medical terminology used to explain and define the symptoms of a patient. For example, as Foucault's translator notes, the title of *The Birth of the Clinic* refers not just to the physical building of the clinic or hospital but to the growth of the discourse surrounding clinical medicine itself (vii).

B.S. Johnson often chose to set his novels within institutions of these types; for example, the school in *Albert Angelo* and the bank and office in *Christie Malry's Own Double Entry*. These institutions are apparently benign, positive and operate for the good of society, but they are also open to abuse from within. *House Mother Normal*, set in a care home for the elderly, illustrates the ways in which disciplinary power is created and maintained within the confines of a physical, material institution. The novel consists of a two-page introduction followed by a section of 21 pages detailing the strictly timetabled events of a single day, as interpreted by each of the eight residents of the home and by the House Mother (whose section comprises 22

pages). The events of the day occur in exactly the same page of

narrative for each of the characters, resulting in a novel that, as

Jonathan Coe notes, can be read "'vertically' as well as

'horizontally'"(24-25). The nine individuals in *House Mother Normal* are

carefully created distinct individuals. Their individuality is created both

by the mock-official detailed records of their own specific medical

history and current condition, and also by the interior monologue that

follows each records, which attests to the fact that each of them

possesses his or her own distinct individual voice.

Foucault states that language makes individuals a subject in

both senses of the word – they are made subject to disciplinary power,

but this power also serves to create them as specific, individual

subjects. The residents of the home in *House Mother Normal* are clearly

differentiated by their own account of themselves and by the "official"

record that precedes each monologue. During this opening section,

each of the residents (and the House Mother) are categorised by a

series of criteria, including their age, their marital status, the condition

of each of their five senses, their capacity for movement and their

mental ability. None of them have identical histories and records and they are rendered as individuals through these accounts. The residents

are also defined as individuals through their personal monologues.

While each of them experience the same event at the same time,

rendered at the same point in the page of their section, their version of

the day's events are all interpreted differently and they all possess

distinct mind styles and memories. Their ailments, listed as

"pathology", are listed in highly detailed, specific medical terminology,

which is, at times, difficult to decode without having a degree of

medical knowledge. This highly specialised language is inaccessible to

the majority of the population, who do not possess in-depth medical

knowledge, and can be viewed as symptomatic of the way in which the

medical profession asserts its authority over patients. The way in which

the House Mother refers to the residents is also telling. As she asserts at

the beginning of the novel:

> Friend (I may call you friend?), these are also our friends. We
> no longer refer to them as inmates, cases, patients, or even as
> clients. These particular friends are also known as NERs, since
> they have no effective relatives, are orphans in reverse, it is
> often said (Johnson, 5).

Although the House Mother professes to reject the more usual, overtly

repressive ways of referring to her charges, her use of the word

"friends" for them is shown to be horribly ironic. While pretending to negate and reject the oppressive discourse used to describe and control the elderly inmates, she in fact callously reinforces the power she wields over them. In addition, she creates a new acronym for them – "NERS" – which simultaneously draws attention to their vulnerability and serves to depersonalise them. The ways in which the residents themselves use language can also be viewed as significant. The use of Welsh, a minority language in the United Kingdom, by two of the residents of the home can be interpreted as constituting a challenge to the power wielded through the discourse of the House Mother – indeed, the only mode of resistance that remains to the incapacitated residents.

There is a clear parallel between the workings of the form of the novel and the techniques used by institutions such as the home in order to control those living within.

As Foucault points out, disciplinary power requires not only enclosure, but a system of partitioning in order to be effective.

> Each individual has his own place; and each place its individual. Avoid distribution in groups; break up collective dispositions; analyse confused, massive or transient pluralities. (*Discipline and Punish,* 143).

This process of identifying an appropriate place in which to situate an individual serves to position them within a structure, the better to control them. Johnson clearly recreates this kind of enclosure and partitioning in the form of *House Mother Normal.*

Within the text, each individual is allotted his or her own quota of space on the page (his or her "own place") and none of the accounts of the residents are permitted to move outside the confines of this space. The account of the House Mother may exceed the framework of the novel, running to 22 rather than 21 pages, but nevertheless, her account remains in its proper place, as do the others. Throughout the novel, each page is headed with a line, the name of the person speaking and the relevant number of the section. The overall effect of the carefully drawn boundaries of the novel is that of reading an official document produced by an institution, perhaps medical notes. Although the majority of the novel comprises the internal monologue of the characters, presenting it in this fashion emphasises the degree of control the institution of the home exerts on its residents, control that extends far beyond their physical environment to their very thoughts and feelings, which are mapped onto the rigid structure of the novel, affording no privacy to the residents.

The form of the novel also demonstrates the ways in which its characters are prevented from forming meaningful relationships with each other. Since each monologue follows on from the last, the reader never gets a sense of conversations taking place between residents. In order to piece together an exchange between two individuals, it is necessary to move forwards or backwards through the text. This reinforces the sense of the group of residents being deliberately isolated and alienated from each other and the possibility of any collective disposition being removed. In this way, the residents are confined, enclosed and partitioned away from each other by both the institution of the care home and by the boundaries of the text itself. In the example of the argument between Ivy Nicholls and Gloria Ridge at the top of page 7, Ivy's account is given first, as she is the more lucid and capable of the two residents in the carefully organised hierarchy of the novel. Ivy's words, spoken out loud, are rendered in italics, whereas her thoughts are depicted in normal type.

> *Here you are. I can't help it if you don't want to work, Mrs Ridge!*
> *Tell her,*
> *Not me. She's the one who makes you, not me.*
> *And you!* The cheek of it!
> *I don't have to do this, you know!* (Johnson, 57).

In order to understand the statement that has provoked Ivy's angry

retort, the reader must move forward in the text and locate the relevant

part of the seventh page of Gloria's account in order to discover that

Gloria has called Ivy a *"slummocky old shit cow"* (Johnson 101).

Therefore, even when the residents are shown in direct conversation,

they are also shown to be irrevocably separated and isolated from each

other. In other exchanges, misunderstandings and mishearings abound,

reinforcing the impression of a lack of communication and

companionship among the residents.

In addition to the institution of the care home, in *House Mother*

Normal, Johnson also subjects the traditional novel form to scrutiny and

criticism, laying down clear boundaries in order to demonstrate how

writing a novel in the form used by nineteenth century novelists, with

invented characters and situations, constrains the writer's enterprise in

a way that he found to be unacceptably dishonest. There was a

considerable amount of debate in Johnson's day regarding the future of

the novel. As Johnson states in the introduction to *Aren't You Rather*

Young To Be Writing Your Memoirs, the form of the traditional novel

had been adequate to convey reality as it appeared to writers in the nineteenth century, but was inadequate to represent what he saw as

the chaos of modern experience.

> Then it was possible to believe in pattern and eternity, but
> today what characterises our reality is the probability that
> chaos is the most likely explanation; while at the same time
> recognising that even to seek an explanation represents a
> denial of chaos (Johnson, 17).

However, Johnson also recognises and acknowledges the contradictions

and limitations of his stated aims in writing, admitting that he was

unable even to explain his concerns to his reader without imposing an

artificial order on his subject, stating that "Even in this introduction I

am trying to make patterns, to impose patterns on the chaos, in the

doubtful interest of helping you (and myself) to understand what I am

saying" (Johnson, 17-18). The conflict involved in attempting to

adequately and honestly represent the chaos and unpredictability of

modern lived human experience without imposing an artificial order

and pattern on it was, as Johnson noted, difficult to resolve.

As we have seen, in the last section of the novel, Johnson

breaks the framework he has established for the characters, allowing

the House Mother to step beyond the limit of 21 pages per character.

> And here you see, friend, I am about to step
> outside the convention, the framework of twenty-one pages
> per person. Thus you see I too am the puppet or concoction of
> a writer (you always knew there was a writer behind it all? Ah,
> there's no fooling you readers!), a writer who has me at
> present standing in the post-orgasmic nude but who still
> expects me to be his words without embarrassment or
> personal comfort (Johnson 203-4).

At this point in the novel, the House Mother speaks with Johnson's

voice, familiar from his other novels, and reveals herself as a fictional

character. As Nicolas Tredell points out, although the House Mother is

undeniably monstrous, she is not merely a grotesque, she is not "a

stable, clear-cut character set at a safe distance from the author and

reader" (128). When the House Mother speaks about the conditions in

homes she has previously worked in, to justify her own actions, she

speaks with authority.

> There are worse conditions and worse places, friend. I have
> worked in geriatric wards where the stench of urine and
> masturbation was relieved only by the odd gangrenous limb or
> advanced carcinoma. Where confused patients ate each other's
> puke... (Johnson, 197).

In fact, several of her examples of the conditions to be found in care

homes appear to have been influenced by *Sans Everything*, a collection

of real-life accounts of abuse in hospitals and homes. Although it is unclear whether Johnson read the full book, a review was found by

Jonathan Coe in Johnson's collection of notes and papers for *House*

Mother Normal. (295-296).

Tellingly, given Johnson's depiction of the House Mother,

several of the witness statements report that doctors and nurses who

are mentally unstable themselves are routinely left in charge of

vulnerable patients. In one account, a male nurse describes how the

staff in the hospital in which he works view their patients:

> I felt that for most of the staff the patients were just a number
> of cogs – and that the introduction of anything new might upset
> the machinery. But surely hospitals should not be regarded as
> factories, or be allowed by any State to function as such? (Robb
> 16).

This example demonstrates how supposedly benign organisations

operate to a strict, disciplined timetable which removes any therapeutic

benefit to those confined within their walls.

The House Mother is the representative of disciplinary power

and status in the novel, a sadistic woman who controls and abuses the

residents in her care, her title a parody of her supposedly maternal,

caring role. Tredell describes the House Mother as "a demonic

inversion of the maternal, nurturing domestic and normative functions

that her title implies (126). Her own behaviour and thought processes are revealed to be highly abnormal, and indeed, her own 'pathology'

states that she is suffering from a malignant cerebral carcinoma

"(dormant)" along with "mild clap; incipient influenza; dandruff"

(Johnson 183). This juxtaposition of these trivial medical conditions

alongside the scientific term for a terminal disease is undeniably comic,

but introduces an important point made by Johnson in the novel.

All the medical complaints of the characters are listed under

the heading of "pathology", in highly specialised terminology which is

inaccessible to those without medical knowledge. On closer inspection,

however, many of these conditions are not diseases as such, but

symptoms associated with the ageing process which most people would

regard as normal. For example, all the residents are listed as having

"contractures", or the permanent shortening of a muscle or joint.

Decreased mobility of muscles and joints is commonly associated with

ageing, and is not generally thought of as a disease, but referring to this

symptom in these terms renders it as specialised medical discourse,

inaccessible to many, and this discourse then becomes a tool for the

operation of disciplinary power – to label the residents as "abnormal"

and to justify their confinement and segregation from society at large.

The question of what is to be considered as "normal" or
"abnormal" is crucially important to *House Mother Normal*. The
residents have been confined to the home under the abusive power of
the House Mother as they do not conform to society's ideals, as their
bodies and minds have deteriorated to the point that they can no longer
carry out useful work. For this reason, they are classified as "abnormal",
and internalise this classification, while accepting that the House
Mother, as a representative of "normality" has the right to exercise
power over them. The concepts of normality and abnormality, and the
distinction that is made between the two, fascinated Johnson. Indeed, as
Jonathan Coe states, his notes for *House Mother Normal* were kept in a
folder marked "NOTES towards a novel on normality". As Johnson
states in the introduction of *Aren't You Rather Young to Be Writing Your
Memoirs?*, his primary motive in writing the novel was to "say
something about the things we call 'normal' and "abnormal'":

> Due to the various deformities and deficiencies of the inmates,
> these events would seem to be progressively 'abnormal' to the
> reader. At the end, there would be the viewpoint of the House
> Mother, an apparently 'normal' person, and the events
> themselves would then be seen to be so bizarre that everything
> that had come before would seem 'normal' by comparison
> (Johnson, 26).

Jonathan Coe finds Johnson's treatment of this theme to be

unsatisfactory, stating that

> In any case, no real link is ever established in the novel
> between abnormality and the infirmities of old age. What is
> supposed to be so 'abnormal' about senility and incontinence
> in the first place?...The nine inmates of this old people's home
> may seem progressively more sad, pitiable and even brave, on
> occasion: but at no point do any of them appear to be
> 'abnormal' (294).

However, in rendering the 'normal' infirmities of old age in medical

terminology, Johnson demonstrates how abnormality and the normal

ageing process are inextricably linked, and in the process, he raises

questions of normality and abnormality that go beyond his stated aims.

Writing in 1989, E. Idris Williams, a professor of public health, raised

the question of "normal" and "abnormal" ageing processes.

> The natural ageing process has been termed senescence and
> shows itself...as 'an increasing probability of death with
> chronological age.' This implies that changes take place in the
> body as time goes by in the absence of recognised disease. Very
> often, however, the process of senescence may also be
> accompanied by disease and one may well affect the other. It is
> still unclear what is the nature of the effect that these two
> processes have on each other and indeed, whether there do in
> fact exist two quite separate ageing processes, one normal and
> the other abnormal (42).

In effect, Johnson's treatment of the "pathology" of the residents of the

home draws attention to the two processes of ageing, and how the medical establishment problematises the symptoms of the normal

ageing process and absorbs them into medical discourse, which is then

used to define them as "abnormal" and to justify subjecting them to the

controlling processes of disciplinary power.

The parallels between the home in *House Mother Normal* and a

prison are clearly apparent, even to the characters in the novel. When

the House Mother refers to Sarah Lamson and Charlie Edwards as her

"trusties"- a slang term used to describe prisoners who cooperate with

their jailers and assist them in managing and controlling fellow

inmates, Sarah reacts indignantly to being so described.

> Trusties, she talks to us as though we were doing bird, indeed, one of these days I'll show her how trusty I am! (Johnson, 13)

Although both Sarah and Ivy Nicholls vow to take revenge on the House

Mother, these are shown to be futile gestures, with Lamson admitting

that she is afraid of her and Nicholls' threats petering out into

ineffective rambling.

> I've a good mind to make complaints about her and this food she gives us, to my friend on the Council, I still have friends- all the treats of our Social Evening, indeed, just like any night is what it'll be, as usual, give me a good book any time, I just want to read (Johnson, 53).

As the House Mother states when she categorises them as "NERs" (No Effective Relatives) at the beginning of the novel, the residents are isolated, they have no relatives or friends from the world outside who might be able to assist them and threaten to disrupt the workings of the disciplinary institution of the care home.

What can be perceived as the most sustained resistance to the disciplinary power exercised within the care home comes from Rosetta Stanton, the most senile of all the residents, whose monologue is written largely in Welsh. At first sight, to a reader unaccustomed to the Welsh language, these words appear to be disjointed, nonsensical utterances, designed to convey the chaos of her disintegrating mind. However, on closer inspection, these fragmented words form a blackly ironic comment on the events of the day and the condition of Rosetta herself. Many of the words translate as adjectives which sharply contrast with the humiliation and degradation of Mrs Stanton's present situation (i.e. *lwcus*, which means "lucky", or *addien*, which means "beautiful"). Since the same event in the novel occurs at exactly the same point across the sections, it is possible to decipher what is going on at the point at which these words occur. By comparing Rosetta Stanton's account to those of other residents, it transpires that

Rosetta's monologue reads *ynad* ("justice") and *noddwr* ("protector" or "patron") at the point at which the House Mother discovers Mrs Ridge's attempt to steal meat from another resident and subsequently physically abuses her by rapping her over the knuckles with the "twitcher." This suggests that Rosetta is, to some extent, aware of her surroundings, although her response to events is somewhat ambiguous due to its minimal nature. Although she could perhaps be providing an ironic comment on the cruelty that she sees enacted by the person employed to care for and to protect the residents, she could equally be interpreted as affirming the House Mother as the protector of the resident whose food is stolen.

The use of the Welsh language in this context is highly significant. Welsh is spoken and understood by a minority of people in the United Kingdom. Thus, by writing Rosetta's monologue in Welsh, Johnson challenges the established discourse of power within the novel, which is predominately written in English. Johnson explicitly links Rosetta, a vulnerable woman who is near death, with the country of Wales and with a culture and way of life that is under threat from Englishness, and in danger of dying out altogether. Rosetta's monologue confirms and reinforces her identity and dignity, and her Welsh words stand as a rejection of the disciplinary power and Englishness espoused

by the House Mother. Johnson himself was highly sympathetic to the

Welsh nationalist movement. Coe quotes an acquaintance of Johnson,

Jeremy Hooker:

> Bryan would have seen Welsh nationalism simply as the
> defence of a different culture, even a different civilisation: a
> defence against the tremendously powerful forces that
> undermine it. I mean the forces associated with Englishness –
> it's not just a matter of language, it's a matter of history and a
> whole spread of uniformity and of things associated with an
> Anglo-American, materialistic way of life (298).

Most English-speaking readers of the novel would be unable to

understand the Welsh words, or perhaps even to realise that they are

indeed words, rather than nonsensical, senile utterances.

House Mother Normal marks a surprising change in Johnson's

approach to novel-writing. In contrast to the strong, determined stance

he had taken with his preceding novels, vowing to write only from his

own experience, in *House Mother Normal*, he is writing from the

varying, distinct perspectives of nine invented characters and using a

fictional situation, although, as we have seen, he drew on real-life

accounts of witnessed abuse. Perhaps, in his view, drawing on these

sources made the invention of characters more permissible. He may have felt that it was acceptable to use these novelistic devices he professed to despise, so long as he acknowledged, finally, that there was "a writer behind it all" (Johnson, 204).

To Johnson, the "writer behind it all" had a responsibility to consider the difficulties and contradictions involved in writing a novel in modern times and to take them seriously. He appears to have considered it almost a dereliction of duty on the part of his British contemporaries that they did not share his concerns, noting that "...there are not many who are writing as though it mattered, as though they meant it, as though they meant it to matter" (Johnson, 29). Part of this seriousness of purpose, for Johnson, was the recognition that the nineteenth-century narrative form was inadequate to convey anything truthful in the twentieth century and a commitment to evolve and regenerate the novel form. Although he saw the continued use of the nineteenth century narrative novel form by modern-day writers as "anachronistic, invalid, irrelevant and perverse", he recognised that there could still be some value and worth in writing novels, if writers were prepared to commit to regenerating the form. As Johnson saw it, there were still some functions the novel could perform more effectively than other forms of media. In the introduction to *Aren't You*

Rather Young To Be Writing Your Memoirs, he states that "the novel may not only survive but evolve to greater achievements by concentrating on those things it can still do best: the precise use of language, exploitation of the technological fact of the book, the explication of thought" (Johnson, 12).

For Johnson, this commitment to evolving the novel form meant that each new work threw up its own paradoxes and problems, which needed to be acknowledged and a workable compromise found, even if a solution proved to be impossible. As Johnson notes, "I feel myself fortunate sometimes that I can laugh at the joke that just as I was beginning to think I knew something about how to write a novel it is no longer of any use to me in attempting the next one" (Johnson, 17). In *House Mother Normal,* the essential paradox of attempting to convey the random nature of experience without imposing an artificial order or pattern on to it, and yet still communicate something truthfully to the reader, results in a novel that exists simultaneously as social commentary and as a commitment to the evolution of the novel form.

Works cited

Coe, Jonathan. *Like a Fiery Elephant: The Story of B.S. Johnson.* London:

Picador, 2004.

Foucault, Michel. *Discipline and Punish.* Alan Sheridan, trans. London:

Penguin, 1977.

---. *The Birth of the Clinic.* Sheridan Smith, trans. London: Routledge,

2003.

Idris Williams, E. *Caring for Elderly People in the Community.* London:

Chapman and Hall, 1971.

Johnson, B.S. *Aren't You Rather Young to be Writing Your Memoirs?*

London: Hutchinson, 1973.

---. *House Mother Normal.* Glasgow: William Collins, 1971.

Robb, Barbara (ed). *Sans Everything: A Case to Answer.* London: Thomas

Nelson Ltd, 1967.

Tredell, Nicolas. *Fighting Fictions: The Novels of B.S. Johnson.*

Nottingham: Pauper's Press, 2000.

"A Sort of Waterfall": Class Anxiety and Authenticity in B. S. Johnson

Joseph Darlington

University of Salford

In the world of B.S. Johnson criticism, the writer's working class origins and attitudes are often referred to as an influential factor within the overall aesthetic of his works. Until now, however, no sustained analysis has been conducted of Johnson's "working classness" and how awareness of these class formations can inform our readings. With access to Johnson's notebooks and correspondence through the British Library's newly catalogued holdings, the possibility of such a reading has emerged. As a beneficiary of Britain's post-war boom it would be tempting to read Johnson as a member of the working class who entered the privileged world of the avant garde due to his exceptional merits. However, a closer look at the evidence does much to dispel the accepted liberal narrative of the post-war era; rather than integration, we find the trappings of class antagonism throughout. Rather than a working class writer clumsily replicating "classless" bourgeois forms – as many critics have inferred - Johnson's work can be read as a negation of the prejudices inherent within the "meritocratic" ideology now hegemonic within British culture.

The primary obstacle facing any academic reading of B.S. Johnson is his works' combination of two approaches – social realism and experimental typography – which for the traditional literature scholar are perceived as incompatible, if not contradictory. Studies such as Glyn White's *Reading the Graphic Surface* and Philip Tew's *B.S. Johnson: A Critical Reading*, however, have made convincing arguments against the kind of approaches that would identify such a contradiction; maintaining that even to treat the two elements as distinct is to misconceptualise their mimetic function. White's thesis is that "disruptions and difficulties at the level of graphic surface which require special negotiation are part of the process of reading the text in which they appear and... cannot be abstracted from it" (21), as a result "the reader responds to [them as they would] to difficulties in the purely semantic message, by taking context and metatext into account"

(22). This is best illustrated in the Johnson canon in the case of the

section beginning "Julie rang on the Saturday…" that conveys a sense

the frailty concomitant with grief both in a single paragraph describing

the news of Tony's death and in the physical act of the reader holding a

lone piece of paper (White, 116). It does, however, also help to

demonstrate many of the moments of existential crisis such as the

"Fuck all this lying!" (167) of *Albert Angelo* and the "But why? All is

chaos and / unexplainable" (82) of *Christie Malry…* both of which

incorporate elements that Tew evokes in his description of the

Johnsonian aesthetic;

> The form and the content through various modes of
> irresolution exemplify the problematic at the core of Johnson's
> aesthetic drive, the admission of, if undialecticised, otherwise
> oppositional elements of life and language that would remain
> divided as forms of impossibility or irresolution ("(Re)-
> Acknowledging B.S. Johnson's Radical Realism, or Re-
> Publishing *The Unfortunates*", 35).

It can be seen that the readings that locate a contradiction within

Johnson's works – positioning them as oxymoronic realist-metafictions

– can be incorporated within more nuanced readings that demonstrate

the compatibility and interrelation of such elements. It is this particular

core of Johnson's writing – where the lived "undialecticised" experience seeks to find meaning – in which its aesthetic unity and narrative strength lies.

The "undialecticised" core of Johnson's writing is engaged with at essay-length by Carol Watts in "'The Mind has Fuses': Detonating B.S. Johnson" through the central metaphor of *The Unfortunates* quoted in her title. She describes it as the critical point of "irascible sense of impasse" that marks Johnson's writing when "the discovery of sometimes incontrovertible limits...might make the lights go out altogether" due to "affective overload" (80). It is an image that recurs both in Johnson's published work, his letters and his notebooks: an overwhelming sense of the "chaos" of the universe that overcomes any attempt at meaningful encounters and narratives. This critical moment is read by a number of critics as a point of deepest existential crisis and modernist alienation. For Levitt it is connected to Johnson's metafictionality: "an obvious heightening of the Romantic obsession with poetic creation but in a more human context" (440). Robert Bond similarly identifies a "vocationalism" – specifically in *Albert Angelo*'s use of architecture – that is "removed from any notion of collective or collaborative labour" and relates to an "ideology of inwardness and individuation" (44). The critical moment in which Johnson breaks from traditional description of a fictional world is presented as escape from the world, as either an elevation or a collapse, which represents a break from the material into the ideal. In a thematic sense, Johnson is following in the long tradition of bourgeois avant garde writing and experiencing a fragmentation of the personality, a descent into the realm of the soul.

The modernist Johnson can be seen to break free of history in both these ecstatic moments and equally through the abandoning of traditional form. For Johnson "the traditional novel...must be avoided because it legitimises *acceptance* of the past" (39), to use Bond's wording. In an interview with Alan Burns, Johnson himself described the "exorcism" that he experienced by writing himself out of the past – specifically his own past – and now "if I want to recall how I felt at the time I wrote *Trawl* I can read *Trawl*, but I don't have to carry it with me. I don't want that stuff popping into my mind" (85). The experience that Johnson conveys is one of an individuation not only distinct from what might loosely be termed the objective conditions of history, but from a personal sense of subjectively experienced history. Identity is rendered sovereign over both time and space. To return to reading Johnson from his influences, he can here be read as drawing on Beckett's disembodied soliloquys in the manner of *Malone Dies* or *The Unnamable*, albeit as a narrative counterpoint to descriptive "realist" scenarios that exist within the same novel. To the read the texts alone it would thus be fitting to consider Johnson a "working class modernist". The negotiation between social documentation and the individual mind within his novels always inevitably favours the latter.

Working Classness and the Value of Labour

As a means of addressing this "modernist" quality of Johnson's writing in regards to his class background without staging a re-enactment of the Brecht/Lukács debate, it will help if we introduce some of Johnson's own ideas concerning the role of politics in literature. Collected in *The Imagination on Trial*, Johnson's interview with Burns sees him defending the fact that "outside writing I'm a very political animal. My novels have generally been written from a political stance but the politics have been very much in the background" (88). For Johnson his contemporary British readers "don't regard books as a way of changing the world" (89); at least not in the way that "the generation of... Welsh miners who educated themselves in libraries [or] the Left Book Club in the thirties" (89) did. The novel is simply an expression of experience, not a means to communicate political points. His political aspirations he channeled into films such as *March!* and *Unfair!,* made with Burns, that "helped a bit in mobilising the trade union movement" (89). For B.S. Johnson, audiences needed addressing directly should a political point need to made – the notion of a "politics of personality" that Johnson may be expressing within his novels does not appear as a conscious concern.

When we look to B.S. Johnson as a working class writer we are therefore not looking to him as a writer *for* the working class as an audience. Neither are we looking to him as a writer *of* the working class who would seek to translate his experience into the bourgeois novel form. Rather, we are simply looking to him as a writer that *is* working class. Although in the post-Blairite era of "identity politics" such an approach may appear reductive, from a historical perspective it locates B.S. Johnson at a critical moment in the expansion of the post-war welfare state. As a member of the working class Johnson nevertheless received a state-funded university education leaving him in a position shared by many of his generation now considered "between classes". The removal of traditional barriers to cultural institutions does not remove class distinctions, however, rather it indicates that class is not a static notion but a historically shifting negotiation of economic

contradictions. Similarly, to seek a static definition of the "working

classness" of Johnson's novels is to miss their vitality as sociocultural

and historical documents; narratological attempts at the unification of

personal contradictions. The "blown fuse" of the Johnsonian mind, its

chaos and confusion, is a violent collision between proletarian

experience and the literary ideology of the bourgeoisie.

Johnson's presentation of class-consciousness does not occur

on an abstract level so much as physically, as part of the symbols

documented during everyday life. *Trawl* presents the genesis of this

class consciousness as part of the young Johnson's wartime evacuee

experience wherein the "dislike of us, the bare toleration of us" (51) by

their *Daily Telegraph* reading hosts is initially considered to be the

sneer of the boss to the worker; "my mother was in fact or virtually a

servant". Taking a moment to remember, however, Johnson then

clarifies that she was "not a servant paid by him, not a servant to him

unpaid, but just of the servant class, to him" (51). When Nicos

Poulantzas writes about class-consciousness he describes the

"autonomous discourse" of the working class "which Lenin called 'class

instinct', which bursts through the envelope that is the domination of bourgeois ideology" (122). Cornelius Castoriadis locates this instinct in

the fact that "everything that is presented to us in the social-historical

world is inextricably tied to the symbolic" (117) and, as such, creates a

"social imaginary" of shared class perspective. In each of Johnson's

encounters with class-consciousness we find elements of this cultural

framework being brought in as signifiers but, more importantly, we

also find class conflict, prejudices, and the concomitant feelings of

shame and resentment "all too aware now of the worst of the human

situation" (*Trawl*, 54). These realisations are presented in an almost

opposing manner to the "blown fuse" epiphanies; the sites of Johnson's

resentful experiences reconstructed in documentary terms. There is a

compact with the reader which assumes awareness of social signifiers

such as *The Daily Telegraph* and a willingness to allow the situation

presented to convey the message. The opposition between Johnson's

modernist, epiphanic style and the novels' moments of social realism

create a certain narrative tension which pulls between class poles.

In terms of a Marxist calibration of class-consciousness as a

means of taking a "class in itself" and organising it into a "class for

itself" there remains very little in Johnson's works; even if we do

consider him in the light of his later Trade Union activist interests. In terms of class in relation to the mode of production, E.P. Thompson

gives perhaps its most practical explanation in the introduction to *The*

Making of the English Working Class (here abridged as "The Making of

Class" in Joyce's anthology);

> Class happens when some men [sic], as a result of common
> experiences (inherited or shared), feel and articulate the
> identity of their interests as between themselves, and as
> against other men whose interests are different from (and
> usually opposed to) theirs. The class experience is largely
> determined by the productive relations into which men are
> born – or enter involuntarily (131).

From this perspective, the professional writer can never be considered

as a member of a particular class at its "purest" consciousness in

conflict with another class; the act of voluntary, self-expressive labour

isn't really alienated, even if it is exploited. The result is the kind of

irony by which Johnson positions Christie Malry in his job as a bank

employee – "he had not been born into money...he would therefore

have to acquire it as best he could... The course most likely to benefit

him would be to place himself next to the money... Christie was a

simple person" (11). The individual that has identified the class in

which they were born into capitalist society yet has not located their

own role ends up replicating the superficial trappings of the ruling

bourgeoisie – being near money – without receiving access to the economic position that would justify that ideology. From the perspective of labour relations the professional writer struggles to be identifiable as "working class" at all.

What Johnson does present us with, however, is an organic replication of this "class instinct" in the way in which he engaged with fellow writers. Famously championing his contemporaries "who are writing as though it mattered" (*Aren't You Rather...*, 29), Johnson revelled in both a sense of solidarity amongst his "class" of writer, and in his ongoing campaign to overthrow the decadent and conservative "Establishment". Alan Brownjohn, interviewed for Coe's biography, described how Johnson's approach to serving on literary committees was to "spend endless time trying to advance the cause of particular writers, and especially trying to get the grants for them" (270). As obtaining grants was "absolutely necessary for [Johnson] to survive in the cultural marketplace" (271), he became very skilled in accessing grants; skills he then used to help the writers he was "very, very loyal" to; "Eva Figes, Alan Burns, Ann Quin, Giles Gordon" (270). Concerning this apparent favouritism, Alan Burns describes later in the biography how Johnson "didn't fight for the writing of people he knew because they were his friends, but maybe they were his friends because he loved the work... partly it was generalship; you see, this was part of his

campaign for the good stuff and we were his allies" (398/399). In terms

of solidarity, Johnson finds his comradeship in fellow experimental

writers who are both equally passionate about their work and equally

poorly paid for it.

Reading through Johnson's letters and notebooks, the

particular class dynamics by which this "campaign" can be seen as

framed are notably similar to the formation of class-consciousness that

is described in his novels; a pattern of rejection with an occasional

success that is formulated as a victory. In a letter from Zulfikar Ghose as

early as 1954, it is clear that Johnson is intimidated by the elite

magazine *The Listener*, leading Ghose to suggest that "editors are

reasonably favourable to good <u>small</u> poems by unknown poets like us"

and long poems are rejected "more because they are long". The

influence of Ghose early in Johnson's career as a fellow self-

mythologiser also plays into this sense of an embattled group of writers

against the Establishment (in a letter marked 9th April 1959, Ghose

literally states that he wants to "discuss an idea... for starting a new

movement in poetry"). Ghose, amongst others that form around

Johnson's *Universities Poetry* circle during his undergraduate years, validate Johnson's writing and locate it within their particular

"movement". That this conception of poetry draws upon the high

modernist manifestos of such avant garde groupings as the futurists

and the imagists is demonstrative in terms of its ability to be at once

rooted in privileged positions and make claims to be anti-bourgeois as a

"higher" culture. That, by 1960, Johnson is writing in his fifth notebook

the rather peevish note, "Zulfikar Ghose, O.M. – in 30 years' time a

smiling, bald member of the establishment" (73), perhaps

demonstrates how his particular conception of a "movement" develops

a more fully oppositional class dynamic. Taking the language of group-

formation from modernist elites, Johnson goes on to apply it in a

manner more befitting one with opposing class interests.

Having attended anti-Vietnam protests together in 1968,

Johnson and a group of close associates started the group Writers

Reading in 1969 which aimed to bring new writing to public attention

through readings and public meetings (Heppenstall, 26). Empowered

by the new sense of organization, Johnson joined a number of other

literary campaigns including the movement to institute Public Lending

Right (Seddon) and – after organizing a recruiting spree described in

letters from Alan Burns – staged an attack upon the Society of Authors for mismanagement and author's falling pay (Figes, 71). As the relatively prosperous 1960s drew to a close and the militant class politics of the 1970s emerged in response to economic crisis, Johnson's politics follow a similar trajectory to that of many in the nation. Johnson and his fellow angry young anti-Establishment fellows engaged in writing experimental yet socially-conscious novels close ranks in the face of a society returning to austerity. His tireless and outspoken calls for writers to receive better pay are as vocal as his calls for "writing as though it mattered", and could even be considered inseparable from one another.

The inversion of a model of personal interest to serve the shared interests of a class does not only occur in Johnson's appropriation of the "movement" model of intellectual favouritism, but also in his continued efforts towards receiving his pay in salary form, rather than per novel. In a practical sense such a wage paid regularly would relieve the financial and emotional burdens that living between lump-sum paycheques creates. But, like all negotiations over pay, there exists the clash of interests over symbolic value also. Rod Mengham, discussing Johnson's demands in relation to his sense of self, suggests that wages would "reflect as far as possible not the market value of the text, but the value of the writer's artistic gifts, of his creative personality" (100). Mengham notes how Johnson frequently deals with his own identity through the metaphors of "debts, loans, mortgages, value" (100). When a wage is paid to the writer, Johnson's novels are figuratively recognised as emanations of an individual and not simply as commodities. A similar formulation of anti-commodificational feeling is noted in the modernist avant garde by Raymond Williams in *The Politics of Modernism*, which he sees as "distantly analogous to the working class development of collective bargaining... yet one of the central points of their complaint against this treatment of art was that creative arts was more than simple labour" (54). For Williams this implies an aristocratic approach to culture that seeks to remove it from the bourgeois world of trade, where for Mengham Johnson can be seen to internalise trade to the extent that he perceives himself as a commodity.

To get to the root of this seeming contradiction it is perhaps worthwhile to turn to Marx's *Capital* wherein the very same contradiction is posited at the heart of capitalism itself. In Chapter 6, opening a discussion of wage labour, Marx describes how the proletarian "must constantly look upon his labour-power as his own property, his own commodity, and this he can only do by placing it at

the disposal of the buyer temporarily, for a definite period of time. By

this means alone can he avoid renouncing his rights over it" (109). For

such a biographically-influenced writer such as Johnson "labour-

power" is entirely enmeshed within the self and inseparable from it. In

asking for a wage, Johnson is then implying that the commodity of the

manuscript is not what he is selling – he is only providing labour-power

for the benefit of a publisher, who in turn claims surplus value in the

sale of the commodity thereby produced: the published novel. Johnson

is asking for a formal recognition of his proletarian status in relation to

the publisher-as-bourgeoisie. However, the market value of a novel is

not dictated by the labour-power invested within it, nor is a writer

beholden to the publisher for access to the means of production in

creating the initial commodity form of the manuscript. Johnson's

imaginative translation of traditional working class labour relations

into the literary industry represents the "blown fuse" of clashing,

oppositional ideologies in the field of economics. Johnson is thrown into

a world of "chaos" not in an existential sense, but as an alienated

worker within an individualistic free market.

From the perspective of the bourgeoisie, for whom individualism is a beneficial ideological model economically, Johnson's demand for payment in the form of wage labour can be taken simply as an upwardly mobile product of the meritocracy not yet acclimatised to their independent position. From a working class perspective, however, the wage system plays a pivotal cultural role (as indicated in the Marx quotation) in the separation of work and home life and, in a related manner, the upholding of self-respect. In his book-length study of "aspects of working class life" *The Uses of Literacy*, Richard Hoggart describes the importance of a "sense of independence which arises from a respect for oneself [that] no one can physically take away"; something that relies upon "keeping the raft afloat" (79), the continuance of which is guaranteed in a consistent wage. What we are encountering in B.S. Johnson can therefore be considered a reaction against the destabilisation of working conditions he experienced in his transition to professional writer. The very form of Johnson's labour is considered suspect, unreliable, and he for practicing it as a means of earning a living. This self-conscious tension is made visible in *The Unfortunates* as he describes his working conditions at his friend Tony's house,

> Long afternoons there, where we would fall asleep, I would, anyway, feel guilty that we were not working as the world was working. June I remember saying something like that, finding it difficult to accept that Tony was working when lazing comfortably in an armchair reading a book. We were working really, it is difficult for others to understand ("Then he was...", 2).

Without any noticeable difference between the activities of work and leisure the writer appears to lack meaningful employment altogether. For a writer like Johnson who is struggling to sustain himself financially anyway, the lack of a clear-cut and stable time and place of work strikes at the heart of his self-respect as a worker and provider. The demand for wage pay is not then a reflection of the actual working conditions of the writer, but an attempt to replicate the superficial conditions of working class existence as a salve for the ideological upset caused by the new insecurity. Wage labour is entirely to do with Johnson's sense of self, but not because he considered himself implicitly valuable – rather, it is because without the confidence imparted to the bourgeoisie through "cultural capital", a secure sense of self is entirely reliant upon the "debts, loans, mortgages" that Mengham identifies as metonymical within Johnson's discourse.

Johnson's particular notions of self-respect, stability and finance extend not only into his personal impression of himself but, perhaps inevitably, also into his attitudes to women. The commodification of sexual relationships exists not only on the most blatant level as humour – for example, the "small kindnesses from Joan" (47) priced at 0.28 in *Christie Malry...* - but also when Johnson attempts to withdraw from the bawdy into euphemism, such as the "usual desperate business" (85) of his father and mother's courtship in *See the Old Lady Decently*. According to Bourdieu's account of sexuality, the fact that Johnson deals in his sexual life in the same manner that he deals in his financial life is only to be expected as part of "an appetite for possession inseparable from permanent anxiety about property, especially about women" (330) is central to the mind-set of all "rising classes". Indeed, for Bourdieu "a class is defined in an essential respect by the place and value it gives to the sexes" (102). There is however, another important historical element to Johnson's attitudes which, although conforming to Bourdieu's analyses, does help to move our conception of Johnson's attitudes out of the area of ahistorical petit bourgeois misogyny and set them in a context; that being the sexual liberation movements of the 1960s and the women's liberation movements of the 1970s. Where the working class subject of Hoggart's 1950s study "still accepted marriage as normal and 'right', and that in their early twenties [for the reason that] what a husband was earning at twenty-one he was likely to be earning at fifty-one" (58), the 1960s saw considerable changes in social conventions concerning marriage and the family. Framed by the widespread availability of the Pill in the early 1960s and liberalization of divorce laws in 1969 and 1973, the "permissive society" may have reshaped certain gender relations yet, as Anne Oakley argued in 1974 (*Housewife)*, the impact of such changes is fairly limited beyond the middle classes. Alan Burns, describing his time as "a member, if not leader" of a group seeking "abolish the family and all the stuff that goes with it" recounted to Jonathan Coe how Johnson would argue against this: "you can't oppose the family, it's all we've got" (405). Johnson's attitudes are not only token for a "rising" member of the working class, but they are also conservative in terms of contemporary mores within his social circle. On top of conflicted class anxieties about the stability of his labour position, Johnson is also in the uncomfortable position of appearing historically backward too. Stuck between a discredited tradition and a rootless future Johnson adopts possessiveness as a means to self-respect.

Johnson's desire to find security and stability in relationships with women is evidenced in his poetry where, as well as money-related metaphors, he also makes use of a range of imagery borrowed from

heavy industry. Collected in *Penguin Modern Poets 25*, his works

"Knowing" and "And Should She Die?" both invest in the love object the

qualities of raw materials to be shaped and transformed through

labour. "Knowing" describes how "knowledge of her was / earned like

miner's pay" (138), functioning on one level as a kind of double

entendre for sexual activity drawing mining and its various strenuous

efforts but – more importantly, considering Johnson's own issues

regarding pay – it also suggests an approach to relationships wherein

commitment and struggle demand appropriate compensation.

Similarly, "And Should She Die?" describes a woman as loved "as Brunel

loved iron" (133), adding an intellectual element to the idea of

mastering the natural and bending it to the will of the designer. The

monetary language by which Johnson engages with women (here

sexual, but elsewhere matriarchal too) is not commercial in the sense of

acquiring women as objects but a more subtle rendering of emotions-

as-investment. Such a conception of relationships is fairly close to the

dead metaphors of modern relationship counselling; "working" at

"building" a relationship from "solid foundations". The particular twist

added by Johnson's distancing effects draws attention to this submerged set of attitudes with a characteristic bluntness that could easily be mistaken for casual misogyny.

"Meritocracy" and Class Anxiety

At the heart of all of this turmoil over groupings, wages, women and, beneath it all, stability anxiety, can be seen the rising ideology of a new social system. Born largely from discourse about democratising elitist monolithic culture – allowing those that excel to rise – and later emphasising the rewards of individual "aspiration", the drive towards expanded access created in post-war welfare state Britain eroded class consciousness (if not actually class difference) in favour of a new "meritocracy". Perhaps aptly (or ironically) for such a postmodern ideological model, the original conceptualisation of "meritocracy" was a satire. Michael Young's 1958 *The Rise of the Meritocracy, 1870-2033*, described a future in which "intelligence and effort together make up merit $(I + E = M)$" (94). Perhaps in reaction to cross-party support for meritocratic principles, Young's satire appears to target the worries of all parts of the political spectrum: the meritocratic future sees the young usurping the old, individuals replacing families, both collective bargaining and inherited wealth are banned, all in the name of a society entirely structured around merit. Pre-Thatcher, many of the anti-social ideas inherent within ideas of "merit" as a signifier of worth remained scandalous and it is important to remember that the social changes that oriented society in that direction were conducted under a different set of ideological and economic imperatives.

The shifting conceptions of post-war class-consciousness lie at the heart of Johnson's own particular contradictory self-image; unable to be truly conscious of himself on pre-existing class terms he "blows a fuse" and turns to the alienation device of ridicule. Johnson's own notebooks are littered with soul searching about his own class position with notes such as this one from *Notebook 4*:

> I am working-class but brought up not to mix with other w/c children – [therefore] I am not accepted either by my own class, or by others. I was always being told I was <u>lucky</u> as I had things my parents never had – this missing the point – no value to me (27).

The "lucky" one that moves out of the working class is doomed to wander between classes, accepted by no-one. It is the kind of thought that would often strike Johnson in tandem with observations about working class life; in this case some old men in a Putney pub, of which he wonders whether they have "known each other since boyhood – or do they only <u>seem</u> to behave the same as ever!" (27). The sense of identity Johnson cultivates is that of the perpetual outsider: working

class to the middle class, but within the working class he feels solitary.

The "meritocratic" element of Johnson's response to class

alienation resides not in a notion of his accessing a "higher" class

position but a more conservative notion of elite culture that, like the

anti-bourgeois modernists described earlier, uses an alternative set of

class-values to more "authentically" appreciate cultural works.

Johnson's earliest notebooks contain a number of notes regarding the

plays he attended and poetry books he was to read – most of them of

the high modernist variety of Eliot, Yeats and Pound. By *Notebook 4*,

however, the class-consciousness separating his appreciation from that

of the academy is becoming present. Of university he states that he

"went to college – gained more specific knowledge of my heroes (ie.

Admired writers) and found they were not the men I thought they

were" (30). In terms of the writers he still admired, it was the audience

that he found disillusioning: "(Arts theatre – first week – hardly anyone

there) A Pinter's play 'The Caretaker' as curtain went up someone said

'another kitchen sink!'" (148). Johnson finds himself excluded from the

culture that would grant him "more specific knowledge" of "admired

writers", but then this culture is found to be one of bourgeois philistinism that would relegate anything from outside its small world

of privilege to the status of "kitchen sink". For Johnson, this was a result

of his own unique experience which was potentially superior, but in all

cases fundamentally different to that of his supposed fellows:

> What I must realise about my university education is that it
> was ... a unique experience which must <u>NOT</u> be generalised
> about, at all costs. And no correlatives can be found for the
> people with whom I was contemporary at Kings (*Notebook 5,*
> 63).

What underpins Johnson's commentary on this passage is the central

contradiction of post-social democratic, "meritocratic" society. The

expanded state and increased access to social provision removes

individuals from traditionally static backgrounds and their cultural

differences have to be resolved on an individual basis, in turn resulting

in a particular distrust of the very system that allowed them to

supersede it. We see Johnson's class position splitting into the two

apparently contradictory aspects of existential self-reflection and

socialistically-minded indignation that run throughout all of his works.

In *Trawl,* Johnson returns to memories of his childhood

schooling as a means of understanding the class aspect of his distrust of

power. He begins with an instance of being caught stealing fruit before

briefly moving on a tangent in which he was accused of being a "THIEF and LIAR and CHEAT" (67) for stealing a Bible from another pupil's

desk after someone had stolen his own. The lesson of the tangent was

that although the young Johnson was in the right, "she had the power,

ah, the power!" (67). From this lesson, the narrative then moves to the

next assembly in which the headmaster complained of a pupil stealing

fruit to eat – "it took some time before I realised he was talking about

me. It was humiliating to realise it" (73). For Johnson, being used as an

illustrative example of bad behaviour before the entire school, masked

behind anonymity in order to appear as an objective correlative to

badness in general, was a clear example of hypocritical "bourgeois

offense. The class war again. They made me their enemy" (73). What

the power structure of the school evoked for Johnson was the injustice

of power and in order to defend himself against this he needed to

reassure himself of the conditions by which he understood himself to

be correct. Johnson describes the feeling as "anxiety about shame" (73);

a sense that one does not know the codes by which those with power

attribute shame, yet being fairly sure that marked differences between

yourself and them – hunger, scruffiness – would be a likely signifier of

shamefulness.

That Johnson goes on to enter the world of educators and the
educated in spite of his "anxiety about shame" does not assume that
education has done its job of socialising him, nor does it imply that
Johnson himself successfully met the demands made of him, rather it
indicates a means by which the internalised anxiety results in an outer
toughness, authenticity and sincerity approximating the "self-respect"
demanded of working class sensibility. For Bourdieu such an anxiety is
related to the autodidacticism by which the working class approach the
bourgeois body of knowledge and, as a result, end up "ignorant of the
right to be ignorant" that "educational entitlement" (329) confers. For
Hoggart the psychological and intellectual effects of class "ignorance"
are reinforced, or perhaps based in, a "physical appearance which
speaks too clearly of his birth; he feels uncertain and angry inside when
he realises that that, and a hundred habits of speech and manners, can
'give him away' daily" (301). As a member of the working class, the idea
of altering behaviour to replicate the manners of the bourgeoisie is
similarly repellent as nothing "inspires a feeling as strong as that
aroused by the person who is putting on 'posh' airs" (86). The result is a
desperate class anxiety in which, despite entering a typically bourgeois
world (in Johnson's case the world of education and experimental

literature), one can never become a full member. One cannot help "betraying" one's origins before the middle class, and yet cannot face "betraying" one's origins by attempting to alter this. As a result, the "rising class" must fall back upon working class notions of self-respect within middle class contexts.

Authenticity and Truth

Johnson's fourth notebook – mostly written during the period of his first entrance into the world of literature following *Travelling People* – demonstrates Johnson returning to questions of his class heritage with an obstinate sense of its own ambivalence. Quoting a television show called "Never Had it so Good" aired "(T.W. 10/3/60)", he picks out the line "working class with money doesn't make you anything but working class" (115). Clearly this line makes an impact on Johnson for its unashamed use of "working class" as an insult. He writes it down in his notebook; clear evidence of the Establishment's true feeling behind the polite mask which has momentarily slipped. His act of writing stands as testimony to that moment of revelation. He writes to himself how "there is no percentage in being an intellectual" (133), and fills his notebook with ideas for working class themed works that revel in a sense of bawdiness commonly used as a disparaging stereotype by

middle class caricaturists: "w/c poem – identification – the quick bonk

on Saturday night After bath" (30), "Play about w/c life (uncut?) with

lurking ballad singer?" (138). It is interesting that this willingness to

engage with ideas of "working classness" emerges between *Travelling*

People and *Albert Angelo* – the first being later declared a "failure" while

the other is deeply concerned with verisimilitude. It could perhaps be

suggested that Johnson's acceptance of himself as both working class

and a novelist at the cutting edge of literary innovation marks the starts

of the "authorised canon", with *Travelling People* representing a petit

bourgeois work that "betrays itself".

A major way in which Johnson felt he "betrayed himself" within

refined cultural surroundings was through his weight. Giles Gordon

described him to Jonathan Coe as housing "huge insecurity within this

vast, elephantine frame. This great figure who was sweating the whole

time – it was like a sort of waterfall... I think he found his body quite

difficult to live with" (391).[1] In fact, Johnson's "fatness" becomes a

recurrent symbol within his works; sometimes referred to with a self-

---

[1] Interestingly, both Giles Gordon and Alan Burns move in their interviews from Johnson's physicality to his wife's beauty – seemingly justifying Johnson's attitudes towards "investment" in women by implying that her attractiveness cancelled out his repellentness.

deprecating humour, such as the title of his film *Fat Man on a Beach*, and sometimes used quite cuttingly, as in some of the excerpts from his pupils presented in *Albert Angelo*: "Slobbery Jew you fat fomf you soppy rabbi. you are a dog" (162), or the origin of the Coe biography's title, "he walks like a fiery elephant" (160). In the section of *The Unfortunates* which begins "Yates's is friendly...", Johnson decides to sit upstairs in a reasonably empty pub and hopes no one will notice his unusual action. Upon approaching the stairs he is met by a mirrored reflection of himself – "St Bernard face...overweight, no, fat" – which becomes a direct embodiment of his social anxiety as he moves "through these contented people, not a single one noticing my fatness, or me" (3): the self is appended as an afterthought.

Taking Johnson's fatness as a physical metaphor for his inability to conform to middle class refinements of taste, it can almost be considered that Johnson's obsession with eighteenth century scatological humour – Swift, Sterne, and (although not mentioned, a perfect intertext) Smollett – is a form of anti-bourgeois protest. Just as he appropriated the modernist avant garde's aristocratic protest for proletarian means, the aristocratic values of opulence, over-abundance and *joissance* flow through Johnson's pastiches. In "Broad Thoughts from a Home", collected in *Aren't You Rather Young to be Writing Your Memoirs?*, parodic poetry such as "crap is crap is crap is crap" is produced by the overfed, piles-ridden Samuel in a celebration of haughtiness, extravagance and the "filthy minded readers" (94) that take pleasure in it. In his seventh notebook Johnson similarly writes down an idea for a story in which a "Fat man who numbers his layers of fat by great meals he has had in the past... tells them to Dr. on death bed" (65). By returning to an aristocratic rendering of obesity as associated with positive traits such as opulence and conspicuous consumption, Johnson is challenging the reading presented under capitalism's ideology of the "protestant work ethic" which associates being overweight with laziness and gluttony. In these flights of humour Johnson is wearing his body with a rebellious pride by celebrating his physical presence in a hyperbolic manner that rings out defiant against what is expected of him.

Of course the kind of carnivalesque celebration which Johnson revels in is not one that will shift attitudes, nor is it one which aims to – it is more along the lines of a refusal to accept the ideological imperatives that society would impose upon him. What is being seen in these lesser known works is reflecting one particular eccentricity of

Johnson's overall iconoclastic approach to literature. The self-consciousness and compensating audaciousness of Johnson's attitude to his weight reflects the same drives he displays when discussing the great Johnsonian bugbear of "truth". Similar to the idea of "experimental literature", "truth" was a term that Johnson himself could never ruminate upon in a manner acceptably academic – appearing more as an emotional plea for authenticity in the face of academic sophism. His most expansive reading of it appears in the essay giving its name to the collection *Aren't You Rather Young to be Writing your Memoirs?*, the ubiquity of which in readings of Johnson has seen it, in White's words, "almost become B.S. Johnson, in his absence" (85). Not only is the writer compelled to tell the truth if they are to practice in good faith, but "I would go further and say that to the extent a reader can impose his own imagination on my words, then that piece of writing is a failure" ("Aren't You Rather…", 28). For Johnson, questions of "truth" in literature then group together a number of debates around verisimilitude, form, language, content, mimesis, and the role of the author and place them all within a seemingly intuitive black-and-white binary of authenticity. That Johnson's application of his truth-mantra overlaps so many questions commonly distinct within academic discourse could very well be why Johnson had such little success

developing it beyond a kind of rebel truism – or a "truth of my truth".

In treating the idea of "truth" as part of Johnson's personal

journey through class-consciousness it is essential to explore the

different attitudes taken to the concept between novels. Its most

striking appearance within Johnson's fiction is in *Albert Angelo* where it

serves as a narratological conclusion in the form of a metafictional

"disintegration" of story. The tone is exasperated, running in one long

sentence without punctuation; "fuck all this lying look what im [*sic*]

really trying to write about is writing not all this stuff about

architecture…. Im trying to say something not tell a story telling stories

is telling lies and I want to tell the truth about me about my experience

about my truth" (167). This is the Johnson of nightmare for one hoping

for a measured explanation; rambling, evasive, brusque and

exasperated with what he sees yet incapable of properly explaining his

exact meaning. Yet this is not the only tone in which Johnson addresses

the question of "truth" in his novels. In *Christie Malry…* the question of

the reader's imagination – one that seems to exasperate the Johnson of

"Aren't you rather…" – is conscripted into comedic service as the author

figure accuses the reader of "investing [his character's] with characteristics quite unknown to me, or even at variance which such description I have given!" (51), before granting a set of allowed freedoms to the reader imagining Christie: "You are allowed complete freedom in the matter of warts and moles particularly; as long as he has at least one of either" (51). Here we have ideas of "truth" and reader response used with a Sterne-like sense of irony – revelling in the "chaos" (to use another Johnson term) that is attributed both to literature and a life without defined teleological meaning. This cosmic irony is both tragic as well as comic, however, as is made clear in the "Last" section of *The Unfortunates* when Johnson considers "but for his illness, death, it seems probably to me that we [Johnson and Tony] might have grown further and further apart, he becoming more academic, I less and less believing academic criticism had any value at all, perhaps saying to him in anger Let the dead live with the dead!" (4). Tony's death, ruminated upon throughout *The Unfortunates* as sitting between meaninglessness and personal meaning – the "truth of my truth" – is validated within the novel only by Johnson's authorial command over it. The questions and debates around "truth" that separated Johnson from his academic friend are resolved by death, just as in *Christie Malry...* they are laughed away as a joke and in *Albert*

Angelo collapse into narrative "disintegration". Evoked in mourning,

laughed at and evaded, "truth" seems to become directly associated

with the Real in a Lacanian sense; imperative to a subject's sense of the

world's cohesion but harrowing, if not impossible to view directly.

However, it is not enough simply to consider Johnson's "truth"

as a naïve synonym for Lacan's "Real". Not only would this reduce

Johnson to evidence in the case for Lacan's unfalsifiable project, but it

would also tell us nothing about Johnson and return us to the bourgeois

position from which he appears to lack the necessary education and

verbosity to engage in literary debate of merit. By drawing a

comparison with Lacan's Real, we are rather tackling a question of

ideological difference and the role that "truth" plays in Johnson's

position as working class literary innovator. If "truth" does take the

position of an absent imperative then each of Johnson's narratives

represent an ideological allegory journeying towards that imperative.

The class aspect of this ideological-cultural production is identified by

Tew in his Johnson monograph when he writes that "formal

experimentalism serves to function as an ongoing perceptual

recognition of the nature of things, for reality and consequently truth

lie at the heart of the enterprise that moves toward a perception of the concrete and material" (11). Johnson's revelatory mode of literary experimentalism privileges "truth" in an anti-academic manner in a violent materialist break from idealism. That his innovations are "directed specifically towards an idea of greater verisimilitude" (Tew, 11) identifies a key distrust of totalising texts and drives the reader toward the material which, like Lacan's Real, can never be reached by the author-figure but can only be approached and directed towards. Functionally, this materialist alienation is conducted in the manner of the physical book as a "constant reminder", described by White as something that "ultimately strikes against the homogenisation of representation and any critically sanctioned surrender to the economy of perception which assimilates texts only to other texts, not texts to life" (117). The truth-imperative is untheorised by necessity as it acts as a call to authenticity and sincerity regarding material conditions beyond the textual. Johnson's materialism is embodied in the "blown fuse" of narrative collapse. The self-perpetuating engines of elite culture are being dismantled from within.

The imperative towards "truth" is not only important due to its role in creating Johnson's particular materialist metatextuality, but also on account of its class-cultural sentiment. The "defiant moral courage"

(314) that it seems to summarise – far more than any theoretical

inclination – returns us to Hoggart's study and another of the virtues

central to working class ideology beside self-respect; sincerity.

Sincerity is relied on "precisely because it does give some sort of

measure in a world where measure is otherwise very difficult to find"

(195). As a virtue, sincerity places value in the subject in absence of any

claims to objectivity. Johnson's "truth of my truth" can be seen to follow

this; implying that academic claims to objectivity are often really

institutionalised subjective values reinforcing a bourgeois

"Establishment". Sincerity links Johnson's many statements on the

importance of innovation within literature too. Alongside the paradigm

of truth seeking in the introduction to *Aren't You Rather...*, Johnson lists

those "writing as though it mattered" – their works representing an

effort, rather than being praiseworthy in themselves – as well as

suggesting that the attempt to write in good faith is also central to the

social good as the traditionalist "cannot legitimately or successfully

embody present-day reality in exhausted forms" (16). For Johnson, the

novelist, "if he [sic] is serious, will be making a statement which

attempts to change society towards a condition he conceives to be

better, and he will be making at least implicitly a statement of faith in the evolution of the form in which he is working" (16). Social concern,

concern for literature as a form, and personal integrity are united in the

act of writing "as though it mattered" and, as such, demand a level of

sincerity that is of-itself valuable beyond academic formalisations of

quality and is rather "true" on the grounds of being the most authentic

that it is possible to be.

Works Cited

Bond, Robert. "Pentonville Modernism: Fate and Resentment in *Albert*
    Angelo". *Re-Reading B.S. Johnson*. Philip Tew and Glyn White,
    eds. London: Palgrave Macmillan, 2007. (pp. 38 – 50)

Bourdieu, Pierre. *Distinction: A Social Critique of the Judgement of Taste.*
    Richard Nice, trans. London: Routledge, 2010.

Burns, Alan. Letter to B.S. Johnson dated 1/7/1973. Held in British
    Library.

---. Letter to B.S. Johnson dated 4/7/1973. Held in British Library.

Castoriadis, Cornelius. "The Social Imaginary". *Class.* Patrick Joyce, ed.

Oxford: Oxford UP, 1995. (pp. 115 – 138)

Coe, Jonathan. *Like a Fiery Elephant: The Story of B.S. Johnson.* London:

Picador, 2004.

Figes, Eva. "B.S. Johnson". *Review of Contemporary Fiction.* Summer

1985. Vol. V, No. 2. (pp. 70 – 71)

Ghose, Zulfikar. Letter to B.S. Johnson, 7/12/1954.

---. Letter to B.S. Johnson, 9/4/1959.

---. Letter to B.S. Johnson, 22/6/1970.

Heppenstall, Rayner. *The Master Eccentric: The Journals of Rayner*

Heppenstall, 1969-1981. Jonathan Goodman, ed. London:

Allison and Busby, 1986.

Hoggart, Richard. *The Uses of Literacy.* London: Penguin, 1992.

Johnson, B.S. *Albert Angelo. The B.S. Johnson Omnibus.* London: Picador,

2004.

---. "And Should She Die?" *Penguin Modern Poets 25.* London: Penguin

Books, 1975. (pp. 133)

---. *Aren't You Rather Young to be Writing Your Memoirs?* London:

Hutchinson, 1973.

---. *Christie Malry's Own Double-Entry.* London: Picador, 2001.

---. *House Mother Normal. The B.S. Johnson Omnibus.* London: Picador, 2004.

---. "Interview with Alan Burns". *The Imagination on Trial.* Alan Burns and Charles Sugnet, eds. London: Allison and Busby, 1981. (pp. 88 – 93)

---. "Knowing". *Penguin Modern Poets 25.* London: Penguin Books, 1975. (pp. 138)

---. *Notebook 3.* Started 23/4/1959. Held in British Library.

---. *Notebook 4.* Started 29/7/1959. Held in British Library.

---. *Notebook 5.* Started 3/6/1960. Held in British Library.

---. *Notebook 7.* Started 1964. Held in British Library.

---. *See the Old Lady Decently.* New York: Viking Press, 1975.

---. *The Unfortunates.* Jonathan Coe, intro. London: Picador, 1999.

---. *Trawl. The B.S. Johnson Omnibus.* London: Picador, 2004.

Marx, Karl. *Capital, Volume 1.* London: Oxford World Classics, 2008.

Mengham, Rod. "In the Net: B.S. Johnson, the Biography and *Trawl*". *Re Reading B.S. Johnson.* Philip Tew and Glyn White, eds. London: Palgrave Macmillan, 2007. (pp. 95 – 103)

Oakley, Ann. *Housewife.* London: Penguin, 1990.

Poulantzas, Nicos. "The New Petty Bourgeoisie". *Class and Class*

Structure. Alan Hunt, ed. London: Lawrence and Wishart, 1977.

Tew, Philip. *B.S. Johnson: A Critical Reading.* Manchester: Manchester

UP, 2001.

---. "(Re)-Acknowledging B.S. Johnson's Radical Realism, or Re

Publishing *The Unfortunates".* *Critical Survey,* 00111570, Jan

1st, 2001, Vol. 13, Issue 1. Web. *JSTOR.* 3 Jan 2013.

Tew, Philip and Glyn White. "Introduction: Re-Reading B.S. Johnson."

Re-Reading B.S. Johnson. Philip Tew and Glyn White, eds.

London: Palgrave Macmillan, 2007. (pp. 3 – 13)

Thompson, E.P. "The Making of Class". *Class.* Patrick Joyce, ed. Oxford:

Oxford UP, 1995. (pp. 130 – 138)

Watts, Carol. "'The Mind has Fuses': Detonating B.S. Johnson". *Re*

Reading B.S. Johnson. Philip Tew and Glyn White, eds. London:

Palgrave Macmillan, 2007. (pp. 80 – 94)

White, Glyn. *Reading the Graphic Surface: The Presence of the Book in*

Prose Fiction. Manchester: Manchester UP, 2005.

Williams, Raymond. *The Politics of Modernism: Against the New*

Conformists. London: Verso, 2007.

Young, Michael. *The Rise of the Meritocracy, 1870-2033.* London:

Pelican, 1958.

B.S. Johnson and Zulfikar Ghose: Friends and Writers. A Conversation with Zulfikar Ghose

Vanessa Guignery

École Normale Supérieure de Lyon – Institut Universitaire de France

B.S. Johnson and Zulfikar Ghose met in the summer of 1959 after the latter invited Johnson to join him as co-editor of the poetry anthology *Universities' Poetry*. They became and remained close friends until Johnson's death in 1973, even after Ghose left for Austin in 1969, where he became Professor of English at the University of Texas. Together they published a collection of short stories, *Statement Against Corpses* (1964) and collaborated on a satirical political piece, *Prepar-a-Tory* (1960). They met regularly when both lived in London, went on long walks, to the pub, to literary events and to the theatre, played squash in Holland Park, held dinner parties at each other's home, and went on vacation to Blauvac in France (in August 1964) and to the Costa del Sol in Spain (in April 1966) with their wives. Their first poems and novels were published around the same time (Johnson's *Travelling People* appeared in 1963; Ghose's *The Loss of India* in 1964); both were reviewers and sports journalists, and both taught in secondary schools when they could not sustain themselves solely by their writing. They frequently exchanged views on literary matters, read each other's work in progress and thoroughly commented on it. The following interview, conducted in Austin, Texas, in April 2013, aims to provide further insight into the relationship between the two friends and into their literary connections.

> *Guignery: The first time you got in touch with B.S. Johnson was in March 1959 when you invited him to become co-editor of the second issue of* Universities' Poetry, *an annual anthology of the best poetry writing by undergraduates from throughout the United Kingdom. In October 1960, you suggested he should become part of the managing committee of* Universities' Poetry. *Could you explain how you worked together, both on the second issue you co-edited, on subsequent issues and on the conferences that were organised? What type of work was involved? How often would you meet? Did you have any disagreements over the selection of poets for* UP2?

Ghose: When I took over *Universities' Poetry*, of which only the first number had been produced before then, I was in my final year at Keele. The co-editors I had chosen—Bryan at King's College, London, Anthony Smith at Cambridge, John Fuller at Oxford—were also graduating that year, which meant that the future of *Universities' Poetry* would be uncertain since all four of us would no longer be connected with a university. I wanted to establish the anthology's future on some secure basis and to exert proprietary control over the choice of future editors. Bryan and I talked about this—not in any organized way, like discussing an item on an agenda, but in the usual random way in which one jumps from one subject to another. Anthony, who had gone to live and work in Bristol, had introduced us to Eric White, Secretary of the Arts Council. A wonderful, generous man, who took a keen interest in the work of young writers, Eric came up with the idea of establishing a managing committee and offered us the Arts Council's elegantly furnished committee room in St James's Square for our meetings. It was Eric who suggested we invite Bonamy Dobrée, professor emeritus from Leeds University, to be our chairman; and later, when Bonamy retired, brought in another eminent professor, Vivian de Sola Pinto, to replace him. We added the poet-editors Howard Sergeant of *Outposts* and Alan Ross of *The London Magazine* to the committee.

Bryan and I did most of the work. As the printer for *UP2*, we had chosen the printer who had done *Lucifer*, the King's College magazine that Bryan had edited. Bryan was particular about the choice of typeface and art work, even the quality of the paper. Such questions of presentation were also my obsession, and the fact that we agreed on the choices that were made perhaps worked unconsciously as a bonding factor in our growing friendship. He did the business transactions, principally with the printer. I corresponded with the editors appointed for the next number(s) and with universities, some of whom we persuaded to sponsor us to the tune of £25 annually, which was not an insignificant sum at the time.

There was never any disagreement over the selection of poems for *UP2*. The four of us had more or less the same taste. We had all grown up in an era in which Yeats and Eliot were still the dominant voices, though, of course, passing variations—as Dylan Thomas's luscious richness and Philip Larkin's long boring yawn that was heard by some at the time as an alluring voice—pulled us briefly astray. Bryan, John Fuller and I met a couple of times and made up a list of poems to choose from. John went away; Anthony was in France, and wrote long letters with his ideas. In the end, the choice seemed unanimous. There was not one poem that one of us wished to include or exclude over which there was any dissenting argument.

Incidentally, mentioning Eric White conjures up the image in my mind of being with him and Bryan at a production of Kurt Weill's *Mahagonny* at Sadler's Wells. Eric received complimentary tickets for arts events and he would invite young writers to attend the performances with him. Bryan and I came out of *Mahagonny* ecstatic and transformed; Brecht's words and Weill's music opened up possibilities for dramatic uses of poetry in which we both were interested. There were other performances to which Eric invited us separately, and I have no doubt that Bryan would be of my opinion, that Eric was thus instrumental in broadening our appreciation of the arts. To have a seat in a box at Covent Garden to watch a Gluck opera surely widened the range of one's artistic sensibility.

Guignery: Could you talk about the poetry scene at that time? In London, the poets of the Dulwich Group, chaired by Howard Sergeant, would meet and read from their work in a pub. There were also readings and discussions taking place at Edward Lucie-Smith's house in Chelsea. Did B.S. Johnson and you regularly take part in these events? Who were the main poets? Did you feel you belonged to a group? Did B.S. Johnson, who sometimes felt alienated, find a place in these groups or did he still feel out of place?

Ghose: The Dulwich Group was not formed as such, it evolved into one. The article you saw in *Scene*[2], a cultural magazine from the early sixties, gives a wrong impression; the photographs are all posed[3]—I'm seen sitting reading while five others are around me listening as if I were reading a gossipy letter to a group of illiterates, and you might notice that I haven't even bothered to remove my overcoat! No one read, or listened to, poetry that way. Journalism is not a reliable witness of the social scene.

Howard Sergeant, who happened to live in Dulwich, had begun the readings at a pub near his house about the same time that Edward (Teddy) Lucie-Smith began to convene a weekly meeting at his house. At first, the Dulwich readings were all organised by Howard. After we got to know him on the *Universities' Poetry* managing committee, he asked Bryan and me to join him to organize some of them. Bryan persuaded Harold Pinter to give a reading, I persuaded Theodore Roethke; later, when we were both associated with *The Observer*, we had the paper do an article, and by then we were being referred to as the Dulwich Group though we had not proclaimed ourselves as one. Many things happen in an informal evolutionary process that history ascribes to some deliberate plan.

Teddy Lucie-Smith's group also did not start out as one though it developed into one and came to be called The Group. In fact, it had started in Cambridge with Philip Hobsbaum who, taking a university

---

[2] "Bards in the Boozer", by B.S. Johnson, *Scene* 22 (6 April 1963): 26-27. This article provides an account of the readings of the Dulwich Group.
[3] The article is accompanied by a photograph of Edwin Brock, reading in the pub "The Crown and Greyhound", and another of "Zulfikar Ghose, a young Pakistani poet, reading to a group including Edwin Brock, Howard Sergeant and Alan Llewellyn".

post away from London, had passed it on to Teddy. Anthony Smith, being a Cambridge man, was part of the original group, and since we had become good friends by 1960 he introduced me to it. The group met on Friday evenings in the drawing room of Teddy's house in Chelsea. Each meeting was devoted to the work of one poet; Teddy would have sent us copies of five or six new poems by the poet, and when we met on Friday, the poet would read the poems one at a time and there would be a critical discussion after each poem. The other poets included Alan Brownjohn, George MacBeth, Peter Porter, Peter Redgrove, Nathaniel Tarn and David Wevill, who all became well known by the middle of the decade. The dominant English poets before us, in the 1950s, had been the Movement poets—Larkin, Kingsley Amis, etc. But attention shifted to the Group when in 1963 Oxford University Press published *A Group Anthology.*

You will not find Bryan in *A Group Anthology.* He was not known until his name burst upon the London literary scene in 1963 with the terrific reviews he received for *Travelling People.* He had published little before then and also had spent months away in Dublin and in Wales while I was moving in a widening London literary circle. Before 1963, he had seemed restrained and shy, his demeanor somewhat deferential. When the reviews proclaimed his genius and made his name famous (I recall one sub-heading in the *Guardian*'s gossip column some time later: PSBS: just seeing those letters was enough for a *Guardian* reader to know the Post Script referred to B. S. Johnson), his naturally vibrant and boisterous personality surfaced, his manner became more confident and he began to assert his ideas like one who has no doubt about the correctness of his thinking. Later, with increasing praise that each new work received, like the awards for *You're Human Like the Rest of Them*, that confidence sometimes appeared to border on arrogance, but I know that he was always sincere and that it was his strong belief in the truth of his vision, which made him state it—his voice rising, his face reddening—with such emphasis, that his auditor mistook the forceful expression as arrogance. When criticizing a poem, as at the Group meetings, his evaluation was objective and fair, and always spoken in the soft and persuasive voice of reason with its implied appeal to tradition as the final arbiter. He was impressed by form and by the brilliance of an image; sometimes, just one sharp image that captured an emotion, was enough, in his estimation, to constitute a whole poem. A few of my early poems— 'Visibility' in my first book is one—were written in this context and when I gave him a copy he usually put an approving check mark next to an image that impressed him as having an original freshness. This is what he endeavoured in his own poems, especially the early ones collected in his first book. No doubt Pound's Imagism and Eliot's objective correlative theory had influenced our thinking, but we saw that images had been central to English poetry since Chaucer; and therefore, when we looked at each other's poems, the first thing we complimented or criticized was the appropriateness of the imagery.

As for the poetry scene: poetry was taken seriously in the sixties; the P.E.N. anthology and the Guinness book of poetry were important annual events, with P.E.N. giving an inaugural party at its beautiful Chelsea house that included a reading from the anthology by the better known poets. Readings at the I.C.A. were well attended. People bought books of poetry, and publishers actually cultivated poetry lists—there were such series as Penguin Modern Poets (in which Bryan, Gavin Ewart and I made up No. 25, which turned out to be the final one), the Macmillan Poets, Cape Editions, and of course there was Faber & Faber to whom many of us sent our first book with the secret hope that T. S. Eliot would launch us as the next Ted Hughes. Apart from the monthly readings in Dulwich, there were readings all over London in public libraries, and indeed all over the country, mostly at universities. Bryan and I gave many readings together. I especially remember going to Leicester University at the invitation of G. S. Fraser, whose writings on modern poetry we both admired and so were pleased to be thus recognized by him. As we left London on the train, I thought Bryan looked somewhat solemn as though he'd received bad news. It turned out that the bad news was that he'd just finished reading the typescript of my novel, *The Murder of Aziz Khan*, didn't like it at all and didn't know how to tell me so, and therefore felt miserable!

An association from that time: there was a limited edition of one of Bryan's books of poems of which the dust jacket portrayed a female with one breast exposed. Bryan was in Better Books and a friend of his said, on looking at the book, 'I see you're going in for single-breasted jackets nowadays.'

Guignery: During that time, you and Johnson would regularly send poems of your own to each other for comments and criticism. Your correspondence reveals that both of you could be quite severe with each other's work. You also had discussions about rhythm, syllabic meter, the use of metaphor... Johnson was apparently interested in the poetry of the Movement, which you didn't seem to care for. What would you say about your respective approaches to poetry at the time?

Ghose: I admired the tight formal structuring of his poems, and shared his interest in attempting such traditional forms as the villanelle. When working on his poems, he looked for the image that would project his idea. We both had an unreserved admiration for Yeats. Also Auden— except for one qualification: Bryan thought that Auden's beautiful line, 'Lay, your sleeping head, my love,' and the poem ('Lullaby') itself were spoiled by the reader imagining a beautiful woman when Auden was addressing a male; Bryan, who insisted that the artist should tell the truth, believed that Auden should have made it clear that he was talking about homosexual love. I didn't think so because the poem was not a confession about a particular lover but an expression of the poet's experience of love. No, argued Bryan, Auden made him see the image of a woman with that opening line and that was a lie.

As for the Movement, I don't think he was deeply interested in it and it would be incorrect to say that I didn't care for it; it would be more accurate to say that we both liked some of Larkin's poems but cared little for the likes of Amis and Wain. The Larkin of *The Whitsun Weddings* impressed both of us as did the new work that Robert Graves was producing, though later when I saw what Europeans like Eugenio Montale and Jorge Guillén were doing I concluded that Larkin was mediocre and Graves superficial. Although I was influenced by the general approbation accorded Larkin and Graves at the time to admire some of their poems, I did think that they were writing as if Eliot and Pound had never happened. Bryan had an idolatrous admiration for Graves. We attended a reading Graves gave at the Arts Council; at the end of it, Bryan introduced himself to Graves and shook his hand while I remained at the back of the hall. I was more interested in Robert Lowell, whose two books, *Life Studies* and *For the Union Dead*, were influential in pointing to new directions whereas the best of Larkin and Graves merely provided an old-fashioned sort of poetical pleasure. Bryan's response to Lowell was more a respectful acceptance of a seemingly major new poet than my keen enthusiasm for an important new voice. That Lowell's later work was disappointing, even trivial, would suggest that Bryan's estimation was the correct one. Almost exactly the same could be said about John Berryman's *Dream Songs*. I was quick to get excited about the new American poetry whereas Bryan remained calmly skeptical. Perhaps there was something about the exuberant tone of American poetry that grated upon English ears. I remember the very pleased, almost gleeful, look on Bryan's face when he told what another English poet (I think it was Alan Brownjohn) who'd said to him that 'Eliot and Pound were barking up the wrong tree'; I can still hear him say that, *barking up the wrong tree*, with the delighted emphasis of one who agreed with the idea.

Guignery: When both of you lived in London, you very often met for long walks, or to go to the pub. Could you tell us more about your discussions? Was literature your main focus, as is the case in your correspondence?

Ghose: Literature was essentially all we talked about. In the first couple of years, 1959-60, when he lived with his parents in Barnes, he would walk across Barnes Common, down Upper Richmond Road, and to St John's Avenue in Putney where I lived with my parents. We would then walk up Putney Hill and go to the Green Man. We barely had more than a few shillings between us and so we usually lingered over half pints of bitter. Our literary conversation was mostly about poets. Later, when he'd moved to his flat in Claremont Square, we met in Chelsea, usually at the Chelsea Potter. Our discussion was invariably about what we were reading and writing, and really was no different from what can be read in the correspondence. We were at the age when one is brimming with ideas, excited with new formal possibilities that create the dazzling illusion that with one's next work one is going to take literature to an unprecedented height, and eager for success; so, we were producing a large quantity of work, constantly evaluating what the other had done, and when we met, talking and talking about it.

> *Guignery: In 1960, B.S. Johnson and you wrote a political satire on modern Conservatism and the upper class called* Prepar-a-Tory, *divided into 12 chapters and including a series of preliminary pieces ("Dedicatory", "Disclamatory", "Invocatory", "Commendatory", "Explanatory"). How did you share the writing? Did you have an outline of each chapter before you started writing?*

Ghose: *Prepar-a-Tory* was written fairly quickly. He began it with an eager gusto to ridicule Harold Macmillan's Tory government and the upper class pretensions of a public-school educated elite. It was a natural, native-born instinct in him whereas I was not infected with the class warfare virus of the natives and for me the satire was more an exercise in writing a special kind of prose. We didn't work to any plan. The thing just took on an organic growth. Sometimes one of us would produce a sketch, the other would rework it, or sometimes one wrote a whole chapter that required no revision. All we needed for inspiration was one more word with the –tory suffix, and off we went into a creative frenzy.

Remember, this was around 1960, when popular culture broke loose. Bryan was very much engaged in the populist revolutionary momentum that was changing the very accent of the English. He wrote satirical sketches with the idea of presenting them in pubs. We tried one or two pubs on Fulham Road, without success, and one thing leading to another, ended up with *Prepar-a-Tory*.

> *Guignery: In the summer of 1961, B.S. Johnson and you spent several days on the coast of North Wales, interviewing people who were looking for the* Santa Cruz, *one of the ships of the Spanish Armada, whose wreck was thought to be in the area. You wrote a story together, entitled 'Hunting the* Santa Cruz'. *How did the collaborative work for that essay?*

Ghose: This was mostly Bryan's work. He did the research and almost all of the writing. It was really his project—he led the way, like Oliver Hardy determinedly marching ahead with some ambitious plan in his mind, while like Stan Laurel I wandered behind, my eyes wide open in confused wonder, not sure where we were headed. I retain three images from that 'collaboration': a red Renault Dauphine, which Bryan drove from London to North Wales; waking up in the hotel bedroom that we shared and seeing him shaving over a large round basin placed on a dresser with a jug of water next to it; walking down the beach where we picked up some objects brought in by the tide and speculated whether or not they bore any connection with the *Santa Cruz*. I also have in my mind an image of a friendly smiling face, that of a local sailor whom Bryan interviewed, but retain nothing of what was said. Bryan was like a present-day investigative reporter, determined to find the facts. The Sunday papers had only recently launched colour supplements (Why do you need a colour supplement, I told *The Observer*, you've got me), and Bryan was hoping to sell the article to one of them and thus create a source of income, with future articles to follow. But no one was interested.

> *Guignery: Both of you were reviewers at the time. Did you often discuss the books you each had to review? Do you have any specific memories of shared enthusiasm for a book or a writer, or of profound disagreements?*

Ghose: Not really. The majority of the books we were given for review were of little or no literary value. Only once was there a book of superior literary worth, when the *TLS* sent me Thomas Berger's *Reinhart in Love*, and I conveyed my enthusiasm to Bryan, but I don't think he was too impressed. I reviewed a lot of slim volumes of poetry for Anthony Smith's Arts Page in the *Western Daily Press*, Bryan did a good many novels for *The Spectator*. Much of the poetry was forgettable and so were most of the novels; but I must surely have made some warmly approving remarks to Bryan when I'd reviewed the latest Larkin or Graves, or discovered some fine lines in David Holbrook; and I do remember Bryan praising Nicholas Mosley. For Bryan, Beckett was the supreme writer of our time. Actually, we didn't talk about his work in any detailed way. After he met Beckett, he would mention some occasional anecdote but we never sat talking about his novels, which, in any case, I had not read. Bryan presented me with the new editions of

Murphy and *Watt*, but I didn't read them until I'd gone to Texas.

> *Guignery: You and Johnson were also sports reporters (on cricket, football and tennis), and you practiced squash together. How important was sport for both of you? Was the sport journalism only a means to make one's living financially or was there a special excitement and significance related to sport?*

Ghose: I'd played cricket since childhood, Bryan played football and tennis. Chance led me to become a cricket correspondent for *The Observer*; and after Bryan had acquired a name as a novelist, his agent George Greenfield got *The Observer* to make him a football correspondent. When I toured India in 1961-2 with the English cricket team, I became friends with the sports editor of *The Times of India*, a man named Niran Prabhu; after I returned to London, Prabhu wrote to me asking me to report Wimbledon for *The Times of India*, and since I was not free during the Wimbledon fortnight I suggested that he hire Bryan instead, which he did.

Though we both needed what little money sports reporting brought us—it was not much since we were paid as free-lancers at a fixed rate by the column inch—we liked the reporting a lot more than our other journalism, reviewing books. We wanted to write sports journalism that did not merely convey information about an event but was a delight to read in itself. I gave a talk, "The Language of Sports Reporting", at a conference at a university (Manchester or Liverpool, I forget which) that was later published in *Readings in the Aesthetics of*

Sport[4]. In it, I suggested that good sports reporting depended upon good descriptive prose that presented the event with imagistic vividness; people should read a sports report, especially on a Sunday by when they knew the result already, not because it was about their favourite team but because it was by a writer whose prose gave them pleasure. It was a point of view that Bryan shared; indeed, he was very particular about what was printed under his name: it made him furious when a sub-editor changed a phrase of his or compressed an idea for reasons of space.

He enjoyed the social aspect of being a reporter and became close friends with the greatest cricket radio commentator and one of the finest sports writers of our time, John Arlott. Several of us would meet before lunch at the famous bar, El Vino's, in Fleet Street and talk for an hour or two while sharing several bottles of Moët et Chandon or Veuve Clicquot. I was there only once or twice, Bryan more frequently.

He was passionate about football, which I didn't care for, and I for cricket, which he found boring. Therefore, we didn't have much to say to each other about sport—whereas with Anthony, who was a fanatic cricketer, I had long chats about the game when I visited him in Bristol.

Bryan and I began to play squash together around 1965 when, newly married, I was living in Norland Square and my wife's brother-in-law, Robert Locke, was in a flat in nearby Holland Park, right opposite the squash court at the Notting Hill end of the park. I'd begun to play there with Robert, and soon Bryan joined us regularly for the

---

[4] H.T.A. Whiting and D.W. Masterson, eds. *Readings in the Aesthetics of Sport*. London: Lepus Books, 1974.

Sunday afternoon at the court. Later, when Robert had gone to Brazil and I had moved to a house in Hammersmith, Bryan and I continued to play at the Holland Park court on Sundays after which we would go to Hammersmith and have tea with our wives. It was at one of these Sundays that Shiva Naipaul turned up with Paul Theroux, something that I'd forgotten until someone pointed it out in Theroux's book about Shiva's famous brother.

> *Guignery: As you recall in your memoir "Bryan"[5], it was on your way to Wembley to watch a women's hockey match in March 1963 that you and B.S. Johnson formed the idea of publishing a collection of short stories together, later entitled* Statement Against Corpses. *Could you tell us more about that particular day and about what prompted that decision?*

Ghose: There's little more to add to what I recall writing in "Bryan", which, however, I haven't reread though you took the trouble to send me a copy: haven't because I can't, it's too emotionally upsetting for me even to think of rereading it. Yes, it was in the tube to Wembley (Betjeman's line, 'The poplars near the Stadium are trembly', always speaks itself aloud in my mind when I say 'Wembley') when we were talking about short stories that we had the dazzling illusion that it was our special destiny to save the short story form. But the only vivid image that survives from that day is the two of us sitting in the press box looking down on the twenty-two short-skirted girls running around excitedly and holding our absorbed attention with their skilful play— well, with more than just their skilful play. We were not exempt from

---

[5] Zulfikar Ghose, "Bryan", *The Review of Contemporary Fiction* 5.2 (Summer 1985): 23-34.

the male presumption of that era that women could not perform so well in sports as men; we'd gone in a light-hearted mood, expecting to be amused and passingly entertained, but instead found ourselves seriously engaged.

> *Guignery: Both of you were originally poets and then you both started writing plays and novels. B.S. Johnson's plays remained, for the most part, unpublished during his lifetime but six of them were published in the anthology* Well Done God! *(2013) edited by Jonathan Coe, Philip Tew and Julia Jordan. You also wrote drafts for plays which, unless I'm mistaken, have not been published. In your correspondence, you often discuss the art of poetry, story-telling, novel writing, but you do not refer as much to drama. Do you recall any specific discussion about the genre? Was it important for both of you to try your hands at drama as well?*

Ghose: We all tried our hands at drama. That's a generalization, I know; but there's some truth to it. Poets were traditionally interested in drama—Dryden, Shelley, Browning, Yeats, Eliot, Auden, Dylan Thomas, Robert Lowell, to name a few principal ones; so had been several twentieth-century novelists—Joyce, Beckett, Saul Bellow, Patrick White, and my friends Thomas Berger and Anthony Smith come instantly to mind. With some of us, if we had had a successful play, like Tom Stoppard did with *Rosencrantz and Guildenstern are Dead*, we would have proceeded to do nothing else but write more plays. More than one novelist has said this to me. Incidentally, just before Stoppard had that success, he had turned to writing novels, producing a fine one titled *Lord Malquist and Mr Moon*, and had he not had the phenomenal success with the play that he did, would perhaps have written more novels.

You're right, that Bryan and I don't say much about drama in our letters. Perhaps this is because any discussion would have been redundant. Representing a small magazine, Bryan received two press tickets and so we saw many plays together. Our opinions usually coincided, which is probably why there's no discussion in the correspondence. The 1950s and 60s were vibrant times for drama: the Berliner Ensemble mesmerized us with productions of Brecht; John Osborne and Arnold Wesker had ushered in a new drama that dealt with the contemporary situation unlike the British dramatists of the previous generation—Terence Rattigan, Christopher Fry, Charles Morgan, and others whose names no one remembers, all very superficial and silly. There was a parade of first-class performances of the great European masters—Ibsen, Chekhov, Pirandello, Durrenmatt—and then something that would be inconceivable today: avant-garde twentieth-century drama—Jarry, Genet, Ionesco, and most importantly, the post-*Godot* Beckett—the period that produced what came to be called Theatre of the Absurd. Sometimes together, Bryan and I saw them all. We didn't have to talk about it, it was something that we breathed, absorbed, and filled us with the ambition to excel in it. My interest was to write drama in verse, and I wrote a play called *Transfer of Power* in which the characters talk in rhyming couplets but the lines are so composed that the audience hears the music of the language without realizing that it's listening to strictly rhyming lines. I believed that Eliot had failed with his pretense of verse in his plays. Lowell's verse drama was no better. And as for Fry, he was forgettable, his verse depended on a stilted kind of language that bourgeois ears heard as 'poetry'. I wanted a natural language that accommodated colloquial speech and yet was highly controlled and charged. Bryan didn't like my play; not because I'd failed to create a credible spoken verse, but because he didn't care for the epic design behind the action. He preferred the Beckettian approach, which I was not entirely thrilled by. We argued about it. I wanted something on the stage that belonged only to the stage, and not something that while written for the stage could also be produced as a film. The phrase that Bryan frequently used to talk about Beckett's plays was 'the human condition', that the dialogue, and often the monologue, was giving us an insight into the human condition.

> *Guignery: You published your first novels around the same time (Johnson's* Travelling People *appeared in 1963, your novel* The Contradictions *in 1966). Were your discussions and criticisms of the novels as thorough as for the poems? Would you always send drafts to each other and make comments that might modify the final version, or were the versions you sent each other already quite close to the definite typescript?*

Ghose: The versions we sent each other were usually the final ones. Bryan invariably had a precise idea of the form his latest novel was to take and would talk to me, often with considerable excitement, of some of the experimental details. For example, he was pleased to conceive the idea of the holes in *Albert Angelo* and talked of the 'solution' he'd found for the 'problem' of how to forecast, or intimate to the reader, a future event while the reader was still looking at pages dealing with the present. He also told me about the double-column passage where the action and Albert's stream of consciousness are juxtaposed.

My most vivid memory of these discussions concerns his ideas for the form of *The Unfortunates*. We were at one of Joe McCrindle's wonderful dinner parties in his house in Kensington Square—these were lavish events with a sit-down dinner for a dozen to twenty guests comprised mostly of writers, literary editors and journalists. After the dinner, Bryan and I retired to a room where we were alone and he told me about the idea for his new novel, which was to be about his friend Tony Tillinghast who had died of cancer. Bryan was excited that he had found a way of mimicking the randomness associated with cancer cells by producing a text which would come as loose pages or signatures that could be shuffled by the reader so that theoretically every reader looked at a randomly arranged text. My job in these discussions was to submit his idea to critical scrutiny, and so I said that there was randomness even in that which was chronologically strictly sequential, and by way of example said that a novel like Dickens's *Great Expectations* presented a character's biography from childhood to adulthood but after reading the novel one recalled the events of his life in a random order; and similarly, I argued, if I were to first read of the events as Bryan proposed to present them then what was to stop me from re-arranging the events in my mind to compose them into a chronological series? My argument was unconvincing and he went on to produce his most original novel.

As for my novels, it is probable that I would not have written any had I not met Bryan and begun to share his obsession with the forms of fiction (and also, during that period, met Thomas Berger, the great American stylist whose genius has yet to be recognized). My first novel, *The Contradictions*, was a direct result of the conversations with Bryan. He liked the form of the mirrored chapters, 'Assertions' and then 'Contradictions', but didn't have much to say about the content. Actually, neither do I. Bryan hated my second novel, *The Murder of Aziz Khan*, because it uses an old-fashioned narrative style. Curiously, the writer who had influenced me when I wrote *Aziz Khan* was John Steinbeck whom I read because Bryan lent me some of his novels, which he liked—which is surprising because Steinbeck was too mainstream to be Bryan's kind of writer. My next novel was *Crump's Terms*, which Bryan saw in typescript and liked a good deal, possibly believing that my schoolteacher Crump was inspired by his Albert, which could be literally true though what influenced my form was the *nouvelle vague* cinema. But *Crump's Terms* was not published in Bryan's lifetime; the first *Incredible Brazilian* was, and the last time we met he told me the sex scenes in it had made him horny—which was a high compliment!

> *Guignery: The two of you and your wives went to Blauvac in France in August 1964. How was your time spent there? You referred in your memoir to the discussions that were recorded and Jonathan Coe quotes from them in his biography. Why did one of you decide to record your literary conversations?*

Ghose: The Château de Blauvac welcomed artists and we assumed we'd be doing some work there. Bryan borrowed the portable tape recorder from his editor at Constable, his first publisher. We went together to fetch it from the house in The Albany, that remarkable little street, like a mews, tucked away on Piccadilly next to the Royal Academy. The person we got the tape recorder from told us that Graham Greene lived in that street. We weren't impressed, didn't consider him a real writer. In Blauvac, we spent the mornings taping conversations or writing, then eating and drinking, then the afternoons driving around the countryside, and the evenings with a lot more drinking and eating. Well, this is a generalized blur of that time and only very partially true, for we spent some whole days away, as when we drove to Avignon one day and to Marseille another to see Le Corbusier's Cité Radieuse (on the roof of which I took some pictures of Bryan). Also, several mornings must have been spent in Carpentras, the nearest town to Blauvac where we could shop for all that food and drink. As to why we recorded the conversations, no particular reason, just thought it was a mod thing to be doing. (That usage of mod is from the 60s. My schoolboys said 'mod' just as today's kids say 'cool').

Guignery: The four of you and the Johnsons' son Steven also went on vacation to the Costa del Sol in Spain in April 1966. Apart from what you mentioned in your memoir "Bryan" (the driving through France, Bryan's eating habits, his fascination for pinballs and soccer machines...), are there specific memories of this trip that you would like to share?

Ghose: I had assumed we'd carry on the literary sort of conversations that we recorded in Blauvac, but that didn't happen. It was more a normal sort of holiday, and all the images in my tranquil recollection are the clichés of being in bars and restaurants and drives in the country. We drank quite a lot, and once quite drunk I wrote a dirty limerick inside the door of a cupboard about the young man from Madras whose balls were made of brass, which caused Bryan to roar with laughter. Steven, nicknamed 'Sausage' by Bryan, was a child, and I retain an image of him at the table, a pudding plate in front of him, his tiny hand flinging the spoon it held at the pudding and making a royal mess. Some time later when I showed Bryan a new poem in which I had the image, 'a messy, a child's pudding plate of a town', he was delighted by the line and wrote 'Sausage!' in the margin.

> *Guignery: After you left for Austin, Texas, in 1969, how often did you come back to London and see him? Would you say your friendship evolved after you left? Were you still reading each other's work?*

Ghose: We kept up a regular correspondence. I sent him the poems I wrote. He was the poetry editor of the *Transatlantic Review* and published some of the poems. He sent me his new poems—his experiments in Wales—and perhaps some short pieces of prose. Nothing evolved: evolution would imply some subtle or radical change, but when I went back in the summer of 1972 and we met for lunch at Wheeler's in Old Compton Street and began with a bottle of Moët et Chandon it was exactly as in the old days.

B.S. Johnson and Maureen Duffy: Aspiring Writers. A Conversation with Maureen Duffy

Melanie Seddon

Centre for Studies in Literature – University of Portsmouth

Maureen Duffy and B. S. Johnson met at King's College London in 1956 when they both enrolled to read for a degree in English Literature. They both contributed to *Lucifer*, the college literary magazine and were part of the wider University of London poetry scene. They later worked together in the Writer's Action Group and campaigned for public lending rights for authors.

Maureen was born in 1933 in Worthing, Sussex and appeared on the literary scene in 1962 with the autobiographical novel *That's How It Was*. Although mainly known for her poetry, her prose work has received critical and popular acclaim. *Gor Saga* (1981) was dramatized and broadcast by the BBC in 1988 as *First Born*, a three-part mini-series vehicle for Charles Dance. She is also the author of 16 plays for stage, television and radio.

Maureen is well known as a humanist and gay rights activist and for her work championing the financial and legal interests of writers. She is currently the President of the Authors Licensing and Copyright Society, and a Fellow and Vice President of the Royal Society of Literature. This interview took place in Fulham, July 2013.

Seddon: In Jonathan Coe's biography of B.S. Johnson there is a reference to you and Bryan as being the only 'serious' students of literature amongst your contemporaries at King's College London in the 50s[6]. Does this match your recollection of that time?

Duffy: Absolutely. We both saw ourselves as being writers, or at that stage, both poets. I don't know whether Bryan had considered writing novels at that stage. I was more interested in the theatre. But we both firmly saw ourselves as poets and I have to say there was a great deal of rivalry between us because we were the two, as you mention, that were absolutely serious about it. It was our lives, our passions and so

---

[6] Jonathan Coe, *Like A Fiery Elephant: the B. S. Johnson Story*.(London: Picador, 2004) p.77

inevitably, in a way, it made a kind of rivalry out of it. I have to admit that I was a bit miffed that Jonathan never asked me for my comments etc. I was very surprised that he didn't contact me. In the little bits on the internet that I have read about Bryan it says he was from a working class background. What exactly does that mean? Because Bryan didn't talk about his background. So what exactly did that mean?

Seddon: I think there's some dispute about that. At the round table discussion hosted by Will Self last year the issue of class came up. Somebody in the audience spoke up and flatly denied that fact saying, 'A load of rubbish. B. S. Johnson wasn't working class in anyway whatsoever and would be laughing at you all here for speaking of it.' So it is clearly a point of contention. It was very surprising, I had never heard anybody challenge that assumption before. It's interesting that you say he didn't speak about his background.

Duffy: No. And Jonathan Coe doesn't deal with it in the book.

Seddon: Well, I think there's a lot about his close relationship with his mother, but the issue of class maybe isn't dwelt upon. I suppose it is something that people have drawn out from the novels themselves.

Duffy: And also the fact that he left school at 16 you know and didn't go on to university until later.

> *Seddon: There is a sense of you both having to fight quite hard to get to that place at King's and it meaning a lot to you. And also after, the sense of it being very difficult to be a writer in London in the early 60s – a struggle due to the financial hardships. Is that something that you think united you?*

Duffy: I think we certainly both felt it. And we were both interested in pushing the bounds of literature. Unfortunately both Eva Figes and Christine Brooke-Rose who were part of the same wave, as it were, died last year so you can't get their thoughts on it. But I think we both felt that the post-war novel had gone back to being middle-brow, middle class and it certainly didn't express my experience and didn't interest me. I think both Bryan and I harked back to the days of Woolf and Joyce. It was the time of the so-called 'Hampstead Novel,' ably written by people like Iris Murdoch and Margaret Drabble. I just felt that had absolutely nothing to say to me and I had nothing to say to it. I'm sure Bryan felt the same. We were part of a wave that was, in my case, partly inspired by continental theatre, people like Beckett and Genet, Sartre and Ionesco who were all doing something different, so called 'experimental'. Every work of art, of literature in a way is experimental. You really don't know where you are going half of the time. I'm sure Bryan felt the same. That was the way we wanted to go – we wanted to jump backwards and then jump forward and fortunately for us there was this feeling at the time, but then of course in the early seventies that all changed again. I had forgotten when Bryan died so I looked it up and it was 1973. In the seventies there was an economic crisis and publishers told those of us who were writing novels (as they often do) that the novel was dead and we should write non-fiction. I did write some non-fiction and Bryan had moved into film, but the nature of film itself became less experimental, less interesting. The mainstream reverted to a much more conventional model and I think that Bryan would have found that very inimical. I wasn't actually personally in touch with him at that time because one of the things that I must say about Bryan is that he really was an old-fashioned misogynist.

Seddon: Yes, I am a huge admirer of his work, but the one thing that jars for me and the one thing that is hard to reconcile is that slight seam of misogyny running through his work. You could excuse it, I suppose, by seeing him as a 'man of his time' or in some ways a man of an earlier time because he seemed deeply old-fashioned in many ways. It's there and you can't overlook it in his work. Did it come out on a personal level?

Duffy: Yes, it was part of why we were sort of in contest. Because I don't think that Bryan thought that women could write seriously and there were occasions when he would come out with something so old-fashioned: a 'bloke-ishness.' So in that sense although we were together we were certainly not in sympathy with each another. Except in the literary sense where we were both looking to expand and break away from the fifties. And also our political views were both left wing. We were both involved to some extent though the fact that I'm still alive and Bryan isn't means that I've been much more involved. But he was involved in the initial campaign for public lending rights, but I think he found it quite difficult that it was basically being run by a coven of women. It could be seen as a limitation on his work. As much as anything I like *Trawl*, I thought it was a great achievement. But it's interesting that as much as anything he drew on characters at King's for his early novels. The Raven was based on a lecturer we had – John Crow; Albert Angelo was based to some extent on a fellow student, Gianni Zambardi whom Jonathan Coe did interview. Quite where Christie Malry came from I'm not sure. Maybe Bryan himself!

Seddon: Were you surprised by his initial critical success? He did certainly have his moment. There is a line in your novel Londoners where it states that everyone wants to be 'fashion's child.' Was that surprising for you or did you see it coming?

Duffy: This is going to sound a bit harsh. Bryan worked very hard at

promoting his work and himself. We used to laugh about it at King's

because we had the English Society which invited poets down to read

and so on and we used to laugh amongst ourselves and say 'At what

point is Bryan going to buttonhole the celebrity?' Bryan would sidle up

and introduce himself and in a way it's understandable because he

came from the sort of background, as indeed I did, where you simply

did not meet literary celebrities. If you go to boarding school and mix in

that particular milieu it is much easier for you to be in contact with

media people and the whole literary world. Whereas if you come from

another background where none of that pertains you have to decide

how to make it yourself or to reject it. Be very determined and bolshy

on your own. There was not that kind of immersion in what is now

called, charmingly, the 'creative industries'. And so you had to

compensate and in some cases you maybe overcompensated in some

ways. Otherwise you were simply not noticed. And I have to say that

there is always male prejudice, Bryan got much more attention than

Christine Brooke-Rose, who got a certain amount, and Eva in her turn. I had a brief flurry of notoriety by publishing works that one critic said were 'scraping the bottom of the barrel' and 'willfully experimental.' And then came the seventies and that was really the end of Bryan. A combination of circumstances was really too much for him. I wrote a poem as I think I told you.[7] I don't know what had happened in Bryan's childhood. As you say he was devoted to his mother. I don't know whether there was a conflict with his father, but he was a very angry personality. The manner of his death was horrific and it was really the act of someone who is deeply angry and depressed. I mean, really in some ways he was like a sort of caged animal and I am quite sure there is much more in his background, his early days, that would have helped occasion that but of course in those days the British as a whole rejected Freudianism and psychotherapy. It was still sort of, 'pull yourself together!' And so there was no way in which he could access any help or kind of understanding for his difficulties. Many of our contemporaries in one way or another suffered through a lack of understanding of the human psyche and its groundings, needs and problems and so on.

---

[7] Maureen Duffy, 'Suicide' in *Collected Poems*, (London: Hamish Hamilton, 1985) p.224

Seddon: Your poem 'Suicide' is very moving and like other pieces written after the death of Bryan there is a lot of anger directed at what was seen as, I suppose, a waste or a very selfish act.

Duffy: A bit of both, but definitely a waste. We both had that experience of being wrenched away from our mothers. My mother was always having to be sent away to a sanatorium[8] to recover and he was evacuated. I don't know about his relationship with his father. And I, of course, didn't have a father except of course in the technical sense. It's a pity really that we had to be rivals. But maybe that provoked the best in us. Who knows?

Seddon: Both of you seem to have seen yourselves as poets primarily and for Johnson there seems to be a real divide between his approaches to these different written forms. Poetry is from the Muse, the Goddess, a romantic spontaneous overflowing of emotion. But the novel, prose is for truth. It's where you put your own version of reality. We seem to be left with two very different vehicles.

Duffy: Yes, I would say there are two different kinds of truth. One is perhaps a very kind of emotional truth, or an attempt to express an

---

[8] Maureen's mother died from tuberculosis when she was 15. Her childhood experiences are recounted in her first autobiographical novel *That's How It Was* (1963).

emotional truth – this is of course poetry. In the 17ᵗʰ century we would just have called ourselves poets, the term 'writer' didn't exist at all. One thing we do share is that we both attempted different media. It's still often unusual. There was this feeling that you couldn't do them all, but it was another way in which Bryan and I rejected literary straight-jackets. And Bryan going into film was a great adventure and yet again, one feels, 'what a waste.'

Seddon: You speak about the group of avant-garde writers that included Bryan and others such as Christine Brooke-Rose and Eva Figes. Did you have the sense of being a group at the time or is this a label that has been imposed retrospectively?

Duffy: No, no we were absolutely trying to do something different as a group, something which had more of its roots on the continent. There was an extremely lively atmosphere at King's and in London University itself of people striving to write. And part of it was fuelled by those of us who were from working class backgrounds. We were the first generation of free secondary education and probably the first in our families ever to go to university. I think that fuels the class based interest in my work and his work and others of that time.

Seddon: Another interesting point of comparison between you is how you both obviously wanted to be writers but you had to hide that fact and instead say that you would go to university and become teachers. There was almost a drawing of the veil over the real dream.

Duffy: Absolutely. And Bryan leaving school at 16, he would have had to. I took the first year of 'A' levels, Bryan probably missed that and that was why he had to make up, going to Birkbeck and doing Latin because of course in those days you could not read English at somewhere like King's without Latin. Bryan would have had to have done that. But we were both intellectually non-conformist and that was why we got 2:2s. As well as the fact that we were intent on being writers and going our own way. We needed to find our own voices.

Seddon: He seems to have been noted for his speech and presence. In your novel 'Londoners'[9] you make reference to a character that is "Johnsonian in girth, and by extension in his speech"...this must be a reference to Bryan?

---

[9] Maureen Duffy. *Londoners*. (London: Methuen, 1983) p.50

Duffy: Yes, it was a sort of combination of Bryan and John Crow. He was hefty and we tended not to be. Remember we had grown up in war time. He was physically bigger than most of us and like me, a couple of years older than our contemporaries. He was a man of presence!

CUT TO A BUNCH OF BANANAS

David Quantick

It's just a coincidence that the first book I ever read by B.S. Johnson –

Christie Malry's Own Double Entry – is the only one of his to be turned

into a full-on movie, but it's an indication of Johnson's tangential

relationship to almost any of the media he worked in that he never had

any of his novels filmed during his lifetime, while the films he did make

(with the possible exception of some of his television work) were

resolutely uncommercial. That's a very long sentence.

I came to Johnson's work, as I said, through *Christie Malry's*

Own Double Entry, which is one of the shortest and the funniest books

in the English language. I own three copies, just in case, all in the

English language, and a fourth copy, which is in Dutch for reasons I

shan't go into here. The movie of Christie, or Xtie, is extraordinary, and I

shan't go into that either yet, because Johnson didn't make it himself;

but it's worth seeing, if only as an indicator that someone (in this case,

the director Paul Tickell) saw something in Johnson's work that was

worth putting on screen. (And in terms of scope and trueness to the author's original intent, it's a braver effort than, say, *A Cock And Bull*

Story, Michael Winterbottom's often hilarious disinterpretation of

Tristram Shandy, one of B.S. Johnson's cornerstone influences and what

would Johnson have made of Rob Brydon and Steve Coogan swapping

Al Pacino impressions? What would Johnson have made of a lot of

things?)

Like almost everyone on earth, I came to Johnson's filmed work

through the screenings Jonathan Coe arranged around *Like A Fiery*

Elephant. Like almost everyone on earth under 60, I had never seen any

of Johnson's films, knew almost nothing about Johnson, had only seen

in fact one photograph of B.S. Johnson (waving the loose sections *of The*

Unfortunates like a fan with a slightly dismissive look on his face, as if to

say, this is a sort of obvious thing to do, why hasn't anyone else done

it?) and so when – if memory serves – the first film was *Fat Man On A*

Beach, I was overwhelmed. There is B.S. Johnson, swaddled in a jumper

that I'm sure my dad owned in the 1960s, beaming his way into shot,

unfolding a tiny camping stool, playing with shells, reciting poetry,

telling stories (is telling lies) and best of all JUMPING UP AND DOWN

ON THE SPOT.

Unlike Johnson, I'm no expert on Samuel Beckett but I bet he

didn't do a lot of JUMPING UP AND DOWN ON THE SPOT. I believe the

finale of *Waiting For Godot* to be a sedentary affair, with no tramps

trampolining. But there he is, the greatest author of his kind ever, feted

by Beckett and Burgess and, I think, Ballard, JUMPING UP AND DOWN

ON THE SPOT. It's a silent comedy moment, enhanced by the use of

Scott Joplin's "The Entertainer", a piece of music everywhere in 1973 as

the theme music to the film *The Sting*. Throughout *Fat Man On A Beach*

there are moments like this, warmth and humour and – with one

exception – no indication of the fact that the film's genial, convivial host

would be dead by his own hand before the programme was shown.

Johnson, as a film-maker, was always at his best when he was

the subject of the film. The documentary supporting *The Unfortunates* is

a much more serious piece than *Fat Man On A Beach*, but Johnson's

presence illuminates some dark material, no mean feat given the

subject matter (the illness and death of a close friend). Modern viewers

will enjoy the subsidiary game of identifying the city where the book

and film take place, with its football team and fantastic Yates' Wine

Lodge, if not the animation sequence where Johnson's friend decays

before our eyes.

Death is the central theme of *You're Human Like The Rest Of Them*, the titular film in the recent BFI DVD collection. I must have seen this film three or four times at pubic screenings, and what's interesting for me is the way audiences have reacted. At first, the bleakness of the theme (we're all going to die, whether we like it or not) somewhat silenced viewers, but recently audiences seem to feel more free to appreciate the film's humour. Lead actor and recurring Johnson favourite William Hoyland is both a harbinger of doom and a death's-head grim comic; he delivers *You're Human*'s notorious joke about *The Archers* as though he were drinking vitriol. Modern audiences will enjoy the scenes set in a real East London school, with a cast of real schoolboys who never auditioned for the Children's Film Foundation.

William Hoyland also stars, if that's the right word, which it is, in Johnson's least popular film, *Paradigm*. On paper, *Paradigm* sounds like *Private Eye* or the *Daily Mail*'s idea of a deliberate parody of an experimental film. A naked man sits on some bits of coloured wood, speaking a made-up language, and ageing visible in each scene, while in the background an annoying electronic hum gets louder and louder. At no point does anyone use the English language or explain what is going on. Criticised heavily at the time if it was mentioned at all, *Paradigm* is actually an emotional and powerful piece, and sees Hoyland at his best as a pure actor.

Johnson's film work was wide-ranging. There's *Unfair!*, a political piece of a slightly simplistic nature. Modern viewers will enjoy seeing Compo from *Last Of The Summer Wine*. There's B.S. Johnson on Dr Samuel Johnson, which is short, witty, and better than anything Alan Yentob or the *South Bank Show* have ever done on anyone or anything. And there's *Up Yours Guillaume Apollinaire!*, which every time I see it, I have to go and look Guillaume Apollinaire on the internet, and am still none the wiser.

Everything on the BFI disc (which is pretty much everything) is worth seeing, and most of it is brilliant, but there's a second side to B.S. Johnson and films, mentioned earlier, by me, in fact. It's the notion of films based on Johnson's work. Most notably, as mentioned, by me, earlier, there's the movie of *Christie Malry's Own Double Entry*, in which Nick Moran plays Xtie with a fantastic numb grace (Moran went on to make *Telstar*, the story of another big one-off talent, Joe Meek. I was going to connect the two, but someone else can do that). With all due respect to Paul Tickell's interpretation, there should and could be more versions of Christie. There's a full-on black comedy in there, authored

or otherwise.

Johnson's other work is similarly suitable to the modern age.

House Mother Normal, his blackest comedy, inspired Beatrice Gibson's

moving *The Future's Getting Old Like The Rest Of Us*, and – despite his

dull reputation among dullards as a "difficult" artist – everything by B.S.

Johnson is eminently filmable. *Travelling People*, his most conventional

novel, would be a brilliant bildungsroman in any medium. *Trawl*,

contemplative. *Albert Angelo*, gritty and funny. Even *The Unfortunates*, a

book in a box in sections to read in any order, is entirely feasible

nowadays. A few years ago, the composer Brian Eno attempted to

create pieces that reordered themselves whenever you played them. In

film, Christopher and Jonathan Nolan's *Memento* is essentially a story in

reordered sections, in fact a very literal reverse telling. Compared to

these works, a chaptered, shuffleable film of *The Unfortunates*, its

themes more important than a traditionally ordered narrative would be

easy to make for computer or DVD.

There's a lot of B.S. Johnson out there (unlike the untalented,

he was always prolific and never obscure) and now his work is freely

available in print, it would be fantastic if it began to seep into other media as well. For now, I do hope you buy the BFI set, if only for the

JUMPING UP AND DOWN ON THE SPOT.

What I Think of Mr. Albert – Experiences of Johnson in the Classroom, as Told by Your Students

Ruth Clemens
(With thanks to Jake Duff and Martin Lindley)

I gained my bachelor's degree in English Literature from the University

of Salford in 2012. During my time as a student I was, of course, given a

comprehensive three-year introduction to the almost complete

literature and critical theory of the English language. My syllabus

encompassed an historical time frame ranging from Beowulf to Ballard

(despite accidentally skipping most of the nineteenth century due to an

exchange year) and as a result of the vast unending nature of cultural

history there were, unavoidably, some texts that were sidelined in

order to make room for the canonical 'big players'. The primary reading

list of my compulsory module *Modernism* was dominated by Woolf,

Eliot, Joyce, and Lawrence. In my first year, *Literary and Cultural Theory*

taught me to examine texts through the lenses of Marxism, feminism,

post-colonialism, and psychoanalysis. It is regrettable but

understandably necessary that, due to the sheer impossibility of

representing every key group of writers of every moment of our cultural history, my professors had to choose a select few based on popularity, accessibility, and the perceived influence and importance of their writing. My degree concluded with the compulsory module of *Postmodernism*, the final installment of the literary chronology. I was excited to be studying the writers whose names had been so mythically adopted by twentieth century pop culture, the books that had achieved cult status amongst young people for their innovation or controversiality. However, next to Vonnegut and Calvino on the set reading list I found a name I did not recognise: B. S. Johnson.

Christie Malry's Own Double-Entry (Picador, 2001) was one of seven core texts for this module. The first assessed piece of work – an essay worth fifteen percent of the final grade – tasked students with analyzing the postmodern traits of a set excerpt of Johnson's novel. In another class of my third year, an elective called *Reading the Page*, Johnson featured heavily again. In recent years a renewed interest in Johnson's writing and an increase in availability of his works means that he is beginning to find a place in the canon of British academia, not just as an example of the quirky literary experimentalism of the Sixties but as a writer who exemplifies the basic tenets of the dominant literary buzzword of the late twentieth century: postmodernism. Of course, it helped that the convener for both of these classes was Glyn White, author of *Reading the Graphic Surface* (Manchester University Press, 2005), which features a chapter on Johnson, and co-editor with Philip Tew of *Re-reading B. S. Johnson* (Palgrave Macmillan, 2007). However, while it is expected for a lecturer to bring his or her research interests to the subjects they teach, White's decision to show undergraduates that Johnson was a key writer of the prevailing cultural style of the last sixty years of British literature was justified. As the academic interest in Johnson grows, so does the number of undergraduates who find 'B.S Johnson' on their semester reading lists between 'H. James' and 'J. Joyce'. I spoke to two former English Literature undergraduates of The University of Salford about their first experiences of Johnson's writing and discovered why they felt that reading Johnson made the ideas behind postmodernism more understandable, accessible, and enjoyable to learn.

"I loved *Christie Malry*," declares Jake Duff, 22. He found the novel a refreshing break from some of the more traditional texts of his degree: "It's the text I engaged with the most, mainly because it used a lot of humour. So in turn I absorbed more of what it had to say." *Christie-Malry's Own Double-Entry* illustrates the core principles of postmodernism in clear, simple, and humourous ways. Its length means that students aren't going to be spending more time on a first reading than an in-depth analysis, and its eponymous protagonist is a bored white-collar worker with a rebellious desire for greatness – something to which a lot of humanities undergraduates can relate. Playfulness with ontological boundaries, the inversion of power structures, and self-reflexivity feature heavily, for example: "You shouldn't be bloody writing novels about it, you should be out there bloody doing something about it" (180) and Johnson's own non-fiction writing provides a succinct commentary of his creative work, making for a useful study aid for students: "Literary forms do become exhausted, clapped out ... That is what seems to have happened to the nineteenth century narrative novel" (Johnson, *Aren't You Rather Young to be Writing Your Memoirs?*, Hutchinson, 1973). Most importantly of all, the novel is intriguing rather than alienating to students, as Martin Lindley, 25, recalls: "Just from seeing the way (Johnson) would play with form, I think of all the texts we studied I found it one of the most interesting. Immediately I wanted to know what was going on; I wanted to figure out straightaway what he was doing. Sometimes when you're given stuff as an undergraduate you can think *'Well, I'm going to read this because it's a set text'*, but I would have read this whether it was on the reading list or not."

The Johnson's inclusion as a text on this module meant that the often overwhelming concepts behind postmodernism were broken down into accessible chunks. Martin had heard about postmodernism before he began the class, but had never studied it. "I think Johnson helped me quite a lot, with Deconstruction especially. Obviously Johnson couldn't have read fully formed Derrida as his translated work wasn't readily available at that point, but in *Christie Malry* the ideas that represent postmodernism are floating around waiting to be articulated". Martin goes on to say how he came to understand Derridan theory through reading Johnson's novel: "I remember the part where Christie is in the basement of his offices and he turns off the power for the whole building. By turning it off he is literally flipping the binary over from powerless worker to in-control boss, undermining the power structure of the whole business. That for me helped me understand Deconstruction." He laughs, "They really liked that in my seminar".

My classmates' immediate reactions to Johnson's novels in the early days of the semester ranged from 'What?' to 'Wow!' to 'Why can't

I find it on my Kindle?'. The fact that so much of his writing cannot be digitised means that students have to engage with his texts in a very practical way. Johnson's experiments with form can provide teachers with interactive teaching aids, from the hole in *Albert Angelo* to the parallel lineation of Albert's inner monologue and his student's jibes. During one particular class, my lecturer brought in his copy of *The Unfortunates* and handed each student or pair of students one of its sections. We each read our assigned part, and then one by one we explained short excerpt we had read to the rest of the class. At the end of the lesson we left the room knowing that as a class we had collectively read and analysed an entire novel in an hour, and each of us had thought about and explained one particular excerpt in depth. We got to personally engage with the interactivity that Johnson had designed for his writing, and it is those classroom experiences that are easily recalled a few months later when exams come around.

Johnson's relevance and usefulness in academia as an illustrative example of a writer of postmodern fiction is evident. Why, then, is Johnson so largely ignored when it comes to compiling the canonical postmodern novels? Johnson's name does not feature on the *LA Times'* 2009 list of 61 "essential postmodern reads", nor is he included on literary social network GoodReads' top 50 "Popular

Postmodern Books" – yet *Christie Malry* does make an appearance as

number 48 of 153 on its user-voted list of "Postmodern Genius". It is

clear, then, that although readers recognise his importance as a writer

of postmodernism he has not yet achieved the cult status held by the

likes of Pynchon and Vonnegut in order to make it as a 'big player'

Evidently, America has held the title of most influential pop culture of

the West for the past fifty years. Unfortunately for British literature,

however, this has meant that a position as the epitomising king or

queen of the postmodernism is reserved for writers who hail from the

other side of the Atlantic.

Many students arrive at university with the vague idea that the

baton for the Great English Language Novel was passed stateside some

point during the first half of the twentieth century. The current A-Level

syllabuses include, overwhelmingly, traditional and naturalistic work

by British novelists from the nineteenth century such as Dickens and

the Brontës and more innovative American novelists from the

twentieth century such as Toni Morrison and D.B.C. Pierre. Although

the Beat Generation may sum up the apathy of a disenfranchised youth

in a consumerist world, Johnson's writing tackles British class issues and the struggle against the powerlessness of an individual's place in British societal structures in ways that American writing cannot. It is important for students to discover that edginess, innovation, and literary experiment are part of the British literary identity too, and to dispel the idea that, when it comes to British prose fiction, adherence to tradition does not equal greatness. Somewhat more worryingly, the twentieth century British innovative writing that is studied before university is overwhelmingly written by and talked about in terms of groups placed on the margins of society such as writers from ethnic minorities and women writers, for example Atwood and Carter. It is obviously important for writers from these groups to be represented in schools. However, it is dangerous to suggest to students that, in the UK, writing which pushes the boundaries of literary normality only comes from the voices of marginalized groups, as this only perpetuates the stereotype that they themselves are pushing at the boundaries of societal normality. Culture and society are symbiotic; a culture in which a white middle class man can be recognised as an important political experimentalist is a world in which a woman can write a novel without her being automatically politicized as a woman writer.

Conversing with Martin and Jake, we found ourselves agreeing about Johnson being unfairly excluded from the canon. Martin senses that an absence of Johnson on Academic reading lists is particularly unfortunate: "I think it's a great oversight, probably. It's interesting on a theoretical level and a formal level, and as a political snapshot of those times as well. So there are loads of reasons for students to read Johnson." Students come to university to have their previous perceptions of writing or readings challenged, and to discover new types of literature which change they way they read altogether. Johnson's place in the undergraduate classroom is perfect for this. He can illustrate the interactivity of the book form in an increasingly digitised age, provide seminar leaders with many opportunities for group study activities, and (most importantly) show that cool doesn't have to be American. Musing over the importance of Johnson's work in a time where the emergence of digital reading devices is challenging the popularity of the book form, Martin adds: "It's unlikely the book will ever go. These are the books that will hold the torch, essentially, of what books can do." When asked how it can be ensured that Johnson continues to find his way onto the reading lists of future undergraduates, Martin replies: "More teaching of Johnson at university and more promotion. *The Unfortunates* is a really interesting idea.

People can get interested in that, it's a really amazing thing to talk about". It is Jake, however, who sums up the importance of the inclusion of Johnson's texts on our *Postmodernism* module most succinctly. I ask him whether Johnson's place as part of our syllabus was justified despite his reputation as a lesser-known writer of literary experiments. "Yeah", answers Jake, "He should be the first thing they have us read. It's a better introduction than bleeding Derrida."

Lacan, Loss, and the Novels of B.S. Johnson

Nick Gadd

There is a long tradition of fiction writers who have experimented with forms – the grandfather of them all is Lawrence Sterne; twentieth century practitioners include Samuel Beckett (B.S. Johnson's hero); Alain Robbe-Grillet and the writers of the *nouveau roman*; James Joyce and his comic successor Flann O'Brien; Jorge Luis Borges. In more recent times we could mention J.M. Coetzee, whose *Diary of a Bad Year* has three voices on every page, a very Johnsonian device, David Foster Wallace, and many others.

Christ, I've never read Robbe-Grillet. Better chuck him in, though, pretend I know what I'm talking about.

'Many others' indeed ... that's nice and vague.

In particular, writers who have experimented radically with chronological sequence include Julio Cortazar, whose novel *Hopscotch* (1966) can be read with the chapters in two alternative orders suggested by the author, and Marc Saporta, whose book-in-a-box *Composition No. 1*

(1963) consists of individual pages in a random order.

B.S. Johnson is very much part of this tradition and his name is cited (for example by Wood 2008: 91 and Barry 1995: 114) as one of the most significant English experimental writers.

It was curiosity about experimental writing that first drew me to Johnson. However after reading his novels what fascinates me is Johnson's motive for experimentation, which is fundamentally different to those of the others mentioned above. Fundamentally, he believed that the novelist has a moral responsibility to

tell the truth – or as he says in the 'almighty aposiopesis' of *Albert Angelo:*

fuck all this lying look what im really trying to write about is writing ... Im trying to say something not tell a story telling stories is telling lies (Johnson 1964:167)

Johnson believed that his experiments with form were necessary because they made his work more truthful. In other words, he believed that

so-called 'realism' was not realistic at all, and

that the only way to be truly realistic was to write something that deconstructs traditional narrative.

So, Johnson is not experimental because abandoning realism is a way to subvert the status quo, as in gay writers like Jeannette Winterson, whose novel *Oranges are not the Only Fruit* "typifies the anti-realist leanings of lesbian/gay criticism" (Barry 1995:148); or because he wants to recreate modern literature by reconstituting the wreckage of the classical past into a new form as in *Ulysses* (Joyce 1922); or because he wants to draw attention to the constructed and alienating nature of capitalist society, as in Brecht's techniques of 'alienation' (Barry 1995:162); but because he believed his experiments with form were the only way that he could really tell the truth about his experience. And in Johnson, the truth that matters is always about **something he has lost.**

Is that really what Joyce was doing? Never mind, it

sounds OK

Given that the concept of 'truth' is a slippery and contested one, it appears that Johnson is advocating a radical subjectivism (the truth is only what I have experienced for myself) weirdly at odds with his actual practice, which complicates the notion of truth existing in one place by introducing contesting voices. For example in the novel *Albert Angelo* he places a character's thoughts in a column next to their dialogue (which of these is 'the truth'?), switches points of view (from 'Albert' to 'I' to 'you'), swaps verb tenses, inserts writings by other characters, quotes other texts, mixes up genres. (Johnson 1964)

Don't forget the 'scare quotes' around the word truth, that looks postmodern

In my view, what Johnson ends up achieving through his use of radical techniques may be an outcome more interesting than the agenda he actually articulates: rather than telling the truth, he problematises it.

Bingo! Nailed it. Onto the next section.

Given Johnson's unswerving commitment to truth in his work, it seems fair enough to ask a few questions about *The Unfortunates* (1969).

For a start, why is the city visited by the protagonist never named? We know from Jonathan Coe's biography of Johnson, *Like a Fiery Elephant* that Nottingham was the city in which he met Tony Tillinghast, the friend whose agonising death is described in the novel (79). We can tell from the description of the city that it is, indeed, Nottingham. Yet the city is never named. Why? What happened to that famous commitment to the truth?

Another question arises from the names of the football teams playing the match that the protagonist has been sent to report. Johnson calls them 'City' and 'United'. Many English cities have teams called City and/or United, but Nottingham does not – its two teams are Nottingham Forest and Notts County. The ground being described, according to Jonathan Coe, is the home of Nottingham Forest. So why fabricate the names of the teams? Why not just say he saw Forest play?

With any other novelist this would not be an issue, but Johnson is the writer who declared, five years earlier, "fuck all this lying" (167). It may seem a trivial point, but it becomes more significant when we consider the match itself.

According to the narrator, the match is "rubbish", and results in a lucky 1-0 win for the team that was outplayed the whole game. Of course, such football matches do happen, and it's not unlikely that Johnson may have been sent to report on one. But the match in question seems to fit a bit too neatly into Johnson's world view – deserving men get abandoned by faithless women, young men get cancer and die before their time, brilliant novelists fail to achieve sales and recognition – and now, on top of everything, the team that deserved to win a football match loses to a fluke goal in the last few minutes. The team is unfortunate, Tony is unfortunate, the narrator is unfortunate ...

As sporting symbolism goes, the metaphor is not bad and we would accept it from most writers, but the suspicion lingers that Johnson has shaped this football match for his own artistic ends, that its symbolic value is what really interests him rather than its truth, that a sparkling 3-3 draw would not have worked for him, the game simply had to be rubbish, one team had to be desperately unlucky, their loss was inevitable, the result of the match was decided, in Johnson's own mind, before the whistle even blew at the start of the match.

And yet -

The point is not really to catch Johnson out in his obviously

unachievable pursuit of truth at all costs. The question (my question) is

whether, reading his work, we feel ourselves coming any closer to

something that we might think is a truth for us. And the answer to this

is surely yes. Of *The Unfortunates*, Johnson says this:

The main technical problem with The Unfortunates *was the randomness of the material. ... The past and the present interwove in a completely random manner, without chronology. This is the way the mind works, my mind anyway ... the novel was to be as nearly as possible a recreated transcript of how my mind worked during eight hours on this particular Saturday.*

... This randomness was directly in conflict with the technological fact of the bound book: for the bound book imposes an order, a fixed page order, on the material. I think I went some way towards solving this problem by writing the book in sections and having those sections not bound together but loose in a box.

... The point of this device was that, apart from the first and last sections which were

marked as such, the other sections arrived in the reader's hands in a random order: he could read them in any order he liked ... In this way the whole novel reflected the randomness of the material: it was itself a physical tangible metaphor for randomness and the nature of cancer (25)

Frank Kermode says that Johnson's experiment was pointless:

These innovations ... kidnap the notion of experiment or estrangement by making it appear that the violation of narrative order in the interests of what he thought of as truth must be blatant. In fact these tricks simply prompt one to ask what the point of this sort of innovation really is (2004).

On the contrary, it seems to me that most readers would understand at once "what the point of this sort of innovation really is" and would recognise that Johnson has hit on a startlingly original solution that makes instant, intuitive sense. Yes – many readers might say – when I think about my disappointing love affairs, things occur to me repeatedly in random order; when I think about loved ones I've lost, the smallest thing can remind me of them, my mind circles around them obsessively, without apparent order and without my control.

Whatever structure Johnson had given the novel, if it was bound together as a book, he could not replicate these aspects of the mind's workings as effectively as he has by keeping the sections loose and in a random order.

Consider, too, the scene in *Albert Angelo* where Johnson places the characters' speech on the left side of the page, and the protagonist's thoughts on the right.

Well, Jeanette Parsons and Lily Stanley, I shall report this affair to the Headmaster. - Ooooh, I'm frightened!	*Who will do fuck-all about it.*

Perhaps there are ways he could have achieved similar effects within traditional prose (oh yes? What would they be, then?) But the method he has chosen is memorable and original

– not to mention funny – at least as much so as the famous scene in Woody Allen's film *Annie Hall* (1975) where, as the characters speak, their thoughts appear in subtitles. It is a kind of visual metaphor – speech one place, thoughts another – which again makes instant sense to the reader and prompts a laugh of delighted recognition.

"I don't know what I'm saying – she senses I'm shallow..."

Johnson's work – novels, poetry, plays – circles obsessively around a
small number of themes, usually connected with the idea of loss.
Jonathan Coe, in his biography of Johnson, *Like a Fiery Elephant*, traces
the beginning of this back to Johnson's experience of being separated
from his parents when he was evacuated from London to High
Wycombe during his childhood in World War Two (47-48). In his early
twenties Johnson had a love affair with a woman who left him for
another man. After the break up (or 'betrayal' as Johnson preferred to
call it) he recycled the experience obsessively in several books – *Trawl*,
Albert Angelo and *The Unfortunates*. He went on about it so much that
his friends had to speak to him on the subject:

*I was still then troubled, burdening them with my troubles, which were
Wendy, still Wendy, or rather the failure to find anyone to replace her, be
as good as she was, or as I had thought she was, had made her out to be,
for my own purposes, no doubt, and no doubt I was boring these two, as I
remember they were rather sharp about it, by then they had had three or
more years of me lamenting the loss of Wendy...*

The Unfortunates is about another loss, too: the death of his friend
Tony, the academic and critic who had given Johnson detailed advice on

his first novel, *Travelling People*. Although Johnson had his reservations about Tony as a critic, it is obvious that the friendship meant a great deal to him and Tony's death was a loss as devastating in its way as Wendy's betrayal.

Jacques Lacan places loss at the centre of his psychoanalytical theory (Nobus, 166-7). According to Lacan, desire always originates in the notion that something crucial is missing, which we must find in order to make us complete as human beings. For Lacan, it is impossible for us ever to completely fulfil our desire – we are always incomplete; we are all 'unfortunates',

> It is, of course, clear that what is supposed to be found cannot be found again. It is in its nature that the object is lost. It will never be found again. Something is there while one waits for something better, or worse, but which one wants (Lacan, 52).

This seems like an almost perfect picture of Johnson. So many people in his life were unsatisfactory: lovers, parents, friends who died too soon; the children he taught, the publishers who wouldn't accept his books, the succession of agents who couldn't secure a better deal for him, reviewers ... His life was all about the loss of things he loved, and yearnings for something better. These desires became the drive for his work, which recapitulated his losses and yearnings obsessively.

In early November, 1973, Johnson's wife Virginia left him, taking their two children. This final loss was too much. A few days later, Johnson committed suicide, leaving a note that read

This is my last

word.

Q. What can creative writers learn from Johnson?

His insistence on finding unconventional solutions to artistic

problems. Johnson didn't want to be called an 'experimental' writer

(19) although that's the burden he has carried to posterity; and he

certainly didn't muck about with form just for the sake of it. He had

something urgent to say, and wanted to find the best, most truthful way

of saying it. Many fiction writers would say they do something like this,

most of us play around with devices like voice, and style, and point of

view, change narrators, or do other things to achieve what Frank

Kermode calls "the violation of narrative order" (2004), but

we still leave the words on the page looking much the same. Johnson

revived typographical and design devices that had not been used since

the days of Sterne, adapted others from his contemporaries – the loose

pages in a box idea originated with Marc Saporta (1963) and invented

some of his own. Johnson's insistence on taking risks in his search for

artistic solutions shows up most novelists before and since as pale and

conservative by comparison.

While **his unswerving belief in something called 'the truth'**

seems theoretically naïve these days, and his contempt for novelists who do things he disapproved of, such as inventing plots and characters, seems bloody-minded and perverse, we must admire (= I admire) the nature of that commitment, the determination to follow through with his convictions, however much publishers tried to dissuade him, however commercially unsuccessful he was. **Johnson was one of those writers for whom writing** *really mattered*. It wasn't something you fool around at, it wasn't a hobby, or a genteel pursuit, it wasn't something you do to get an academic qualification. It was something to be pursued with absolute conviction and determination and moral integrity and if you weren't prepared to do that, then forget it (Coe, 453-4).

His commitment to excavating **his own experiences**, even (or especially) the painful ones, the ones which centred on a lack, a loss, a 'betrayal' gives his work what Johnson would undoubtedly call 'truth'. What would I call it? Something like: a recognisable representation of a man who was constantly, and unsuccessfully (like all of us) seeking to make himself a whole person in the Lacanian sense. Johnson is the dominant character in many of his own novels and he is always desiring, always grieving, always disappointed: this makes his characters resonate with us very deeply (because as Lacan taught, we

all want something, don't we?). The constant repetition of those

desires, the endless obsessive circling around them, is made all the

more effective by the unconventional devices he uses to emphasise

them. Has the idea of loss ever been more poignantly communicated in

a work of fiction than by the notorious hole   cut in page 149

of Albert Angelo?

But with all this banging on about lack and loss, the danger of forgetting

(or understating) just how *funny* Johnson's work is: the way he can

make you almost cry with laughter, sometimes, because you recognise

it, what he's saying, that frustration or incongruousness, that absurd

contrast between what we say we are, what we pretend to be, and what

we really are (if that's not an essentialist view); all right then, given the

constructed nature of the self (the fact that essentially there is no

essence, ha!) the way that Johnson plays on

that for comic effect, draws attention to the contrasts between what

goes on, on the

outside, and what is happening on the inside – like his school teacher in

Albert Angelo

I'll give you a list of books which you can borrow from the library – the school library may have some of them – is there a school library? Have you seen a pen? A Parker fountain pen, black ...	*Using it when this class came in. Making notes from Frankl. Oh Christ, went out of the room! Some bastard has knocked off my pen! Oh, oooohr! Makes me feel ill, ill.*

And this, too, is part of what makes Johnson's work so resonant, so

recogniseable (*truthful*, he would say); because it's NOT just about how

you never forget your losses, you never stop thinking about that love

you lost, or never even had in the first place for chrissakes,

and it could crush you if you let it, because you never forget, never stop

cursing your bloody awful luck, and you are never complete, although

all of that is true; it's also about how you carry on, you find humour in

things, there are always things to laugh at, even in the

darkness (like Beckett) and there's a connection in that, isn't there, we

connect when we laugh, when we think, yes, that sort of thing has happened to me, I'm like that too, I'm just like that. And isn't that sort of connection between a writer and a reader, isn't that what we want to achieve as writers, *isn't that really the whole point?*

So here's what I learned from the work of B.S. Johnson.

Absence. Loss. Lack. Betrayal. Rejection. They're good things.

Because if you *haven't* suffered, if you haven't been betrayed, if you haven't supported that unfortunate team, that rubbish football team that attacks the whole game, dominates the whole game and STILL MANAGES TO BLOODY LOSE, if you haven't had a publisher tell you 'it's not quite right for our list', if you haven't missed out on the job you wanted, if you
haven't seen the one you love go off with someone else, lost a friend, missed the boat, missed the train, missed the goal, failed the test, bombed out in the interview, dropped the ball, if you are not one of The Unfortunates ... then you are complete, and if you are complete then life is perfect, there's nothing missing, there's nothing to desire, and **if you desire nothing you have nothing to write about.**

Thank you, Bryan Stanley Johnson.

Works Cited

Barry, Peter. *Beginning Theory.* Manchester: Manchester UP, 1995.

Coe, Jonathan. *Like a Fiery Elephant: The Story of B. S. Johnson,* London: Picador, 2004.

Coetzee, J. M. *Diary of a Bad Year.* Melbourne: The Text Publishing Company, 2008.

Cortazar, Julio. *Hopscotch.* London: William Collins, 1966.

Johnson, B. S. *Albert Angelo.* London: Constable, 1964.

---. *Aren't You Rather Young to be Writing Your Memoirs?* London: Hutchinson, 1973.

---. *Trawl.* London: Secker and Warburg, 1966.

---. *The Unfortunates.* London: Panther Books, 1969.

Kermode, Frank. 'Retripotent'. *London Review of Books,* 26 (15), 2004.

Lacan, Jacques. *The Seminar of Jacques Lacan, Book VII.* New York: Norton, 1992.

Nobus, Dany, ed. *Key Concepts of Lacanian Psychoanalysis.* New York: Other Press, 1998.

Saporta, Marc. *Composition No. 1.* Richard Howard, trans. New York: Simon and Schuster, 1963.

Wood, James. *How Fiction Works.* London: Jonathan Cape, 2008.

From the Girl in the Book

Henry, the weight of your desire
is more than I can bear. I fear
that I am more real than most,
less real than all, of my making
not yours, some of the good,
but all of the bad: and not yours,
in that I can only be unfaithful.

Conditions of Dying

Some sage has it that we die three times:
when we breathe our last,
when we're claimed by earth or fire
and with the final uttering of our name.

I can bear the thought of one and two,
and three must be my legacy to you.

Poetry by Jeremy Page

WRITING AS THOUGH IT MATTERED

Reviews

Johnson, B.S. *Well Done God!: Selected Prose and Drama of B.S. Johnson.*

Philip Tew and Julia Jordan, eds. London: Picador, 2013.

Juliet Jacques

Edited by Jonathan Coe, Philip Tew and Julia Jordan, *Well Done God* aims to represent the "enormous totality" of his work. Collecting several of B. S. Johnson's television and theatre scripts, along with selected journalism and all of *Aren't You Rather Young to be Writing Your Memoirs,* and published by Picador to commemorate the 80th anniversary of Johnson's birth, the texts in *Well Done God!* are unified by Johnson's key themes: the conservatism of British culture; the dishonesty of narrative fiction and the limits on authorial communication; and the inevitability of death.

One of the last things he wrote, the introduction to *Aren't You Rather Young* opens the book and summarises many of Johnson's signature ideas about literature, efficiently setting the tone for both that volume and this collection. Noted for its list of authors "writing as though it mattered", including Samuel Beckett and Angela Carter as well as less feted contemporaries such as Ann Quin, Rayner Heppenstall and Christine Brooke-Rose, this manifesto also repeated Nathalie Sarraute's assertion that literature was a relay race with the baton of innovation passed through generations, and his belief that for a novelist to tell stories was inherently disingenuous.

The second section provides an intriguing insight into how Johnson worked his preoccupations – and a more diverse range of influences than is often acknowledged – into a dramatic form where he could not so directly alert his audience to the machinations of an author. These plays, rarely or never performed with several appearing in print for the first time, are only intermittently successful: the best, a radio script entitled *Down Red Lane,* is a darkly witty dialogue between a hungry diner and his belly, exploring the inability to resist harmful desires and their consequences with more economy and levity than his other scripts.

The "Short Prose" section is most interesting, revealing plenty of Johnson's travails with the literary and film industries and his efforts to unionise its producers. His willingness to expose his own working conditions and to criticise his idols, particularly Beckett, is commendable – the revelatory qualities of these pieces, along with the BFI's fascinating DVD compilation of his films and television programmes, may finally allow the 'enormous totality' of Johnson's work to be appreciated by more than a small group of hardcore acolytes.

Johnson, B.S., dir. *You're Human Like the Rest of Them: The Films of B.S. Johnson*. London: BFI Flipside, 2013. DVD and Blu-ray.

Nicholas Middleton

Before I begin this review I must admit to something that will sound like sacrilege for *BSJ: The B.S. Johnson Journal* readers:- I've never read any of the man's books. His obscurity in the public sphere is not something readers of this journal may want to acknowledge, but nevertheless he remains an underrepresented author. I make my apologies in advance. This new Blu-ray release, a collection of Johnson's work in the moving image, looks set to change that and now people outside literary circles can discover B. S. Johnson's legacy through a different medium.

In common with all in the British Film Institute (BFI)'s Flipside series of discs, *You're Human Like The Rest Of Them* is a sumptuous double disc affair with a thick pamphlet, written by Jonathan Coe. Not knowing quite what to expect, I tentatively put on the first film, inwardly grinning at the author's abbreviated pen name (not to mention his surname as a punchline to that joke.) This is a normal reaction and simply the way the British treat their intellectuals; sincerely, but always with the capacity for ridicule - this time I make no apologies. The compilation is by no means complete, but over the short period he was making films, Johnson managed to work in many different film forms and this disc is representative of that. Whilst never a natural filmmaker in my opinion, Johnson was keenly excited by the possibilities of the medium and his fascination with pushing the boundaries of documentary and the short film is immediately obvious.

There is a surrealistic red thread that's visible from his earliest work on this disc, *You're Human Like the Rest of Them* (1967) through to his final film *Fat Man on a Beach* (1973). In the former, Johnson

experimented with making a cut at each actor's line, a device that

highlights the existential trauma of the main character. *Fat Man on a*

Beach will be familiar to Johnson completists, having been available on

YouTube for years. In the film, Johnson deconstructs the documentary

form, detailing the "deceits of filmmakers" in a relaxed and playful

piece to camera. Both these films display an anarchistic approach

reminiscent of the French filmmaker Jean Vigo (whose artistic career,

interestingly, was also cut tragically short), and with shades of the

absurdism of Lindsay Anderson. Obsessed with breaking the fourth

wall, almost all the films on the disc depict a character looking at the

camera - as if Johnson wants to literally step out of the screen and

confront you personally to wax lyrical about Welsh poetry.

Not all of the films hit the mark. *March!* is an overlong and dull

film made for the ACTT union, and *Paradigm* (1969) is, to my mind, an

experimental short that should have never left the cutting room (with

apologies to David Quantick!). The BFI would have done well in

including the very funny *The Smithsons on Housing* (currently available

on YouTube), a documentary directed by Johnson about the British

architect couple whose utopian vision of a glorious socialist Britain is hilariously juxtaposed with complaints from tenants about vandals.

Johnson's approach to the craft of filmmaking derived much of its inspiration (unwitting or not) from Soviet-era film theory, largely ignoring developments closer to home, such as the British Free Cinema movement of the '50s. His style flirts with many techniques whilst never firmly aligning itself with any one dialectic. Indeed, it might be said that only in his final film did Johnson acknowledge there even was a dialectic surrounding cinema, literally holding a mirror up to the camera. None of the films here seem much indebted to cinematic history then, and it will come as no surprise that most of them have a literary starting point instead. Through his affectionate tributes to Samuel Johnson, Beckett, and Apollinaire, Johnson's creativity and humour must have shone like a lighthouse in the fusty fog of postwar BBC programming. The literary nature of these films is problematic for those attempting a reading of his brief career in the moving image, though. Perhaps we would have seen a development in Johnson's interest in the dialectics of cinema had his career not been so short, ours is only to speculate.

In many ways, Johnson was the quintessential English intellectual - overlooked in his day and marginalised in the mainstream after his death. He was a contradiction; a writer who made films, he wanted to speak to the mainstream through the medium of television whilst pushing at the margins of the avant-garde, to simultaneously reach out to the world and recede into the shadows. Unlike one of his more famous books, he was not easily placed into a box. I can imagine now how Bryan Stanley Johnson might have chosen his pen name - it's a perfect encapsulation of how in the contradictory world of B.S. Johnson, the high-brow and the profane live side-by-side. This double-disc release can only serve to increase exposure to Johnson's work and that's a fine thing. Though he was not a groundbreaker in terms of the medium itself, Johnson can stand proudly in the pantheon of British intellectuals who forayed into film. I think it's time to buy that copy of *Christie Malry's Own Double-Entry* now.

Danielewski, Mark Z. *The Fifty Year Sword*. London: Palgrave, 2012.

David Hucklesby

Originally published in a limited run by De Bezige Bij in 2005, Mark Z. Danielewski's *The Fifty Year Sword* presents an evasive and inventive take on the ghost story. The reader is invited to accompany the forlorn seamstress and divorcée Chintana to a party, celebrating the fiftieth birthday of the unrepentantly adulterous Belinda Kite. The arrival of a disquieting storyteller and the ominous box he bears brings forth a tale of misdirection, a sinister motive, a quest for revenge and a weapon to kill fifty years. In its original form – an unusually tall and narrow print novella of 100 pages featuring twelve illustrations by Peter van Sambeek – *The Fifty Year Sword* presents a chilling work of linguistic and narrative complexity. Its five unnamed narrators, identified only by the colour of their quotation marks, dance their way through a fractured but finely woven narrative bearing wordplay and allusion on themes of cutting, sewing, and the threads which bind us together.

Whereupon
Chintana's thumb
abruptly began to sore a
little

and she
felt bleak,
     as if a thousand

vengeances upon
vengeances were dicing
her
suddenly
     into hail.
     (Danielewski, 62)

The newest publication of *The Fifty Year Sword*, through

Pantheon in October 2012, constitutes a comprehensive rearrangement

of the original text, reduced in its physical dimensions, and extended in

length to more than 280 pages. Now puncturing and perforating the

dust-jacket from the inside out, Danielewski's incisive reimagining of

the ghost story bears its original narrative and formal unorthodoxy, in a

new configuration which scratches and claws against its binding.

Reproductions of stitched, pin-pricked and paper-cut illustrations now

scatter the storyteller's journey across its valleys and peaks, and sunder

its form in a swirl of breeze and blades. The opening of the storyteller's

box becomes a sequence of black-printed pages in landscape

configuration, textually, visually and physically mirroring the lifting of each portentous latch. Here, *The Fifty Year Sword* is reincarnated with a wide range of textual, spatial and illustrative forms which lend a new swiftness to its reading.

> There nothing moved
> and I was
>
> alone.
> Anything that had
> stumbled
>
> upon such
>   a wideway of grey
> grief had not
>
> chosen
>   to stay.
>   (Danielewski, 90)

Moving nimbly between a more sparse typographic spacing and concrete textual arrangements, the physical and visual alterations made for this edition of *The Fifty Year Sword* create a tense and addictive reading experience all of its own. Both discursive and expositional of the spatial and tactile qualities of its own paper construction, this new iteration of Danielewski's dark novella both presents and physically embodies the telling of a story which is as fragmentary as it is bound by a taut thread.

Patricia Lockwood. *Balloon Pop Outlaw Black*. Portland: Octopus Books, 2012.

Joseph Darlington

Balloon Pop Outlaw Black is Patricia Lockwood's first published poetry

collection. Her poems have appeared in *Poetry, The London Review of*

Books, and *The New Yorker* amongst other renowned journals, although

it is probably for her internet presence that she is known best.

Tweeting under the handle @TriciaLockwood, she brings her own

brand of sweary, sexy and surreal humour to the loose affiliation of

users collectively known as "Weird Twitter" and, between tweets, has

written poetry catch-ups to the show *Mad Men* for ThingX.tv. As a poet,

Lockwood captures the novelty, joy and playfulness which represent

the best of the web's possibilities and posits a new earnestness and

humour in the face of tired postmodern irony.

At the heart of *Balloon Pop Outlaw Black* is an almost surrealist

tension between metatextuality and narrative poetry. One of the finest

examples of this is the long poem "The Quickening"; a staging of Jonah

and the Whale in which the characters are made up of writing, books and stories. The imagery is bursting with transformations that fall dizzyingly between the literal and the metaphorical; "the whale is an intellectual, she has designed a book that even whales can read; a book that surrounds them" (64). The story might know its own fictionality yet, rather than simply being knowing, its self-awareness acts as a springboard into new imaginative spaces. Sometimes, such as in "Old Green American Says I Grew A Law Last Night", these spaces seem recognisable; a distinct vision of America where anything is possible, the "children all outline their hands and a flock of chickens appear". Other times we are placed firmly in allegory: forests where "Good Climbing Trees Grow Us" or in "fact mines" (78) watching "Children with Lamps Pouring Out of their Foreheads". The phantasmagoric imagery sparkles like early Brautigan but with a poetic concision and intimacy.

Stylistically, the collection interweaves prose-poem and free-verse techniques with a close eye for pacing. Much like Lockwood's inimitable tweeting style, a density of meaning is conjured without recourse to ostentation and often with surprising results. Chasing tightly-packed images down the flowing lines, the pure enjoyment is distinctly contemporary. Rather than retire into pensive moods and ennui, this is poetry which holds its own amongst the welter of mass-media entertainment instantly available to the modern audience. It throws poetry into the new world of communication culture, confident in holding your attention and delivering what no other medium can offer. If we're to ask who is writing as if it matters today, any measure of modern poetry would be amiss not to mention Patricia Lockwood.

Patricia Lockwood's new collection, *Motherland Fatherland Homelandsexuals*, was released in May 2014, published by Penguin.

Contributors

Ruth Clemens graduated from the University of Salford in 2012 and currently works as an accounts assistant at a solicitors where she firmly upholds the glorious principles of double-entry bookkeeping

Kate Connolly has recently completed an MLitt in Modernities at the University of Glasgow. Her research interests include Johnson and his contemporaries, in addition to modernist writers such as Katherine Mansfield, Leonora Carrington and Fernando Pessoa.

Joseph Darlington is co-editor of *BSJ* and part-time lecturer at the University of Salford. He specialises in the history of British experimental novelists in the Sixties but has also published on literary depictions of terrorism, Doris Lessing and Anthony Burgess.

Nick Gadd is a Melbourne novelist, the author of *Ghostlines* (2008).

Vanessa Guignery is Professor of Contemporary English Literature at the École Normale Supérieure in Lyon. She published a monograph on B.S. Johnson entitled *Ceci n'est pas une fiction* (2009), and translated Jonathan Coe's biography of B.S. Johnson into French (2010).

David Leon Higden, Paul Whitfield Horn Professor Emeritus at Texas Tech University, is the author of *Time and English Fiction, Shadows of the Past in Contemporary British Fiction,* and the recent *Wandering into Brave New World.* At present, he is completing *Mind the Gap: A Study of British Counterbooks.*

David Hucklesby is a PhD candidate based in the Centre for Textual Studies at De Montfort University. His research compares innovative works of print literature of the Twentieth and Twenty-first Centuries, and identifies the ways in which such works reflect and react to the technology of other narrative media.

Juliet Jacques is a freelance writer whose book on Rayner Heppenstall was published by Dalkey Archive Press in 2007. Her work has been featured in *The Guardian, New Statesman, London Review of Books* and various other journals and publications.

Nicholas Middleton is a documentary filmmaker based in London, England.

Jeremy Page is a poet and founding editor of *The Frogmore Papers*. His latest collection of poems is *Closing Time* (Pindrop Press 2014).

David Quantick is a writer and broadcaster whose credits include the HBO series *Veep*. He has been a B.S. Johnson fan for more than half his life now

Melanie Seddon is a tutor and doctoral researcher at the University of Portsmouth. She is also co-editor of *BSJ: The B. S. Johnson Journal*.

Printed in Great Britain
by Amazon